The Passable Cook

The Diary of

Hanna Karlina Morland

J. W. JESSER

Dedication

This book is dedicated to
Frances Blado Jesser.
Thank you, Gram, for your love and dedication.
You always believed in me.

The Diary of Hanna Karlina Morland
De Smet, South Dakota

Monday, February 27, 1937
My 17th birthday!

I came home from school to find Mom and Dad sitting at the table and staring at a box from Aunt Karlina. It was addressed to me. I wanted to open it right away, but I decided to wait until David came home so he could join in the fun.

I sat with them a bit and stared at the box, but could not stand the anticipation, so I went and pounded out some hymns on the piano.

Mom started supper. Dad tried to read the paper, but several times I caught him looking at the box over the top of the paper.

He counted the postage and told us how many kroners it cost to send it. He looked at the dates that were stamped on it and declared that Aunt Karlina had sent it in October.

Finally! David came home from the farm. I cannot believe how that 19-year-old he can dawdle.

Mom said we had to eat supper first.

The table was cleared, tea and cookies were served. Dad took out his pen knife and slit the box open.

On the top was a letter, in Norwegian, of course. It was written in such a shaky hand that I asked Dad to read it.

It greeted me with a blessed Christmas. Aunt Karlina had recently moved to Bergen to live with her son. The family home, in Grimstad, was closed up. Her son hopes to return someday, but with job shortages, he felt he needed to stay in Bergen. As she was packing her belongings, she saved several things that she thought that I would like to have and some to share with the family.

The first thing we unwrapped was a packet of letters *Bestemor* and *Bestefar* had sent to her over the years. I handed them to Dad. He took them with cloudy eyes.

A hymnal and New Testament that belonged to my great grandfather were next. A silver brooch with dark purple stones, the note with it said that Grandmother had given it to her when they left Norway. Mom said it as a klumpenklache, or some such, it was to hold the top of your sweater together. A collection of knitting needles, a paperweight made from whale bone, and a knife for David with a handle made from a reindeer antler. A small wooden doll carved by my grandfather for Aunt Karlina. A pair of mittens. She said that it was the last pair of *votter* that she would ever make. Her hands did not work well any longer.

And lastly this leather diary. I shall record my days from now on.

Dad smoothed out the newspaper wrappings to read later.

We sat and stared at the treasures. Mom served more tea.

We talked of the grandparents and their bravery of leaving all they knew to come to South Dakota.

After supper, The Girls and Henry surprised me by making ruckus on the front porch, stomping and singing. Marilyn brought a cake and Henry had some ice cream. It was a wonderful birthday.

Monday, March 22, 1937

We woke up to wind but no snow. Walking home from school was tough. Dad and David made it home just before the storm hit late this afternoon. It is now snowing with vengeance. After supper, I got all caught up in Algebra.

Tuesday, March 23, 1937

The blizzard continues. We are enjoying our snug house. This morning, I curled up with a book and cup of tea. I did help with folding laundry and some of the cleaning.

This afternoon, I started translating the letters I got from Aunt Karlina. Here is one that I particularly liked.

May 12, 1933
Rural Route 2
De Smet, So Dak
USA

Hilsen fra Amerika til min kjære svigerinne over havet,
My dear sister-in-law, Karlina,

> *It is with great sadness that I write you this day. The sky is heavy with dark clouds and my heart is filled with sadness.*
>
> *Karl, your brother, and my dear husband has left this earth. It was a short illness, and he did not suffer. During the last few months, he had lost his strength. It was most difficult for him to sit and watch others work. He was only 72.*

Karl and I moved back to the farm 3 months ago. It was good to return home. Karl spent his days on the porch watching the day go by.

The years have been good to us. I am reminded of the first day that we arrived. We were young and strong. We bought a farm with something the Americans call a relinquishment. The farm had a well and small barn, which became our home that first year. Karl built a pleasant house for us. I now can see the results of our work, a summer kitchen, a large barn for the cows and horses, a sheep barn, and a chicken house. We planted gardens and an orchard.

The precious furutrær *seeds that you gave me, the day we left Grimstad, sprouted, and grew. I have seven stately trees surrounding the house. As I step out of the house, I can smell our Norwegian forests.*

My children are all well. Our eldest son, Edvard served in the Great War in France. He lives with me. The war has made him weary of life.

Ernest, our second son and his wife Margaret live in the house in town now. They have two strong, intelligent, and is this Bestemor too proud when she says beautiful children. David is 15 and reminds me so of Karl with his big ideas and hearty laugh. Hanna is 13 with fiery hair that would make any Viking proud. She has a temper to match. She reminds me so of myself at that age. Her father will have to fight off the boys with a big stick. She can be very studious and quiet and plays the piano and violin. She does not have the patience to sit and learn Hardanger.

Ellinore is married to a quiet man and lives in Canton, South Dakota. She scorns our Norwegian ways and insists that we call her Julia. She will only cook American food and does not speak Norwegian. I must confess that I find it all very like a fly buzzing around my head. I refuse to speak to her in English. She has three lovely girls, Veronica 13, Gloria 11, and Celeste 7. Can you imagine such American names? I do not see them nearly enough.

The years and miles continue to separate us. My heart longs for you. If we do not ever see one another in this life, we will meet again in heaven, where my dear Karl waits for us.

Love,
Johanne

Wednesday, May 12, 1937

I aimed at the light pole, but the rock hit her squarely in the middle of her forehead.

All of The Girls turned and gasped, "Hanna."

Mrs. B. turned and said, "You Nazi."

I ran into the house, slammed the door, stomped upstairs, threw myself on my bed and cried.

I cried from anger.

I cried from humiliation.

I cried because I hate her.

I cried because I was glad that the rock hit her.

And I cried because I am such an awful person.

Mom called me for supper. I ignored her. I knew what was happening when Dad's feet made their slow steady ascent up the stairs.

He knocked and I ignored him. He came in and sat in my desk chair. I turned to face him. From the look on his face, I knew that he knew all about it.

"Mrs. B. is a difficult person to endure. We will probably never understand why she says and does what she does. Now it is time to wash your face and come to supper. This will all be forgotten after you send her a note of apology."

He didn't even ask for my side of the story.

I was just standing there, in front of our house, talking with The Girls. I scooped up a handful of gravel and started throwing the pebbles at the light pole. I missed it most of the time. Mrs. B. came walking up the sidewalk and I hit her squarely on the forehead.

My note will say:

Mrs. B.,

I am sorry the tiny rock hit you, I was aiming at the light pole.

Hanna Morland

Wednesday, June 10, 1942
Old Settler's Day

It was such a gloomy day; the sun was shining, and the blue sky was filled with fluffy white clouds. My heart aches.

Private David Morland and Private Henry Norgaard walked in the parade with a group of young men, home from basic training.

The crowd cheered.

Mom refused to go to the parade, saying she had to make supper.

I stood between Dad and Uncle Edvard. Dad had tears trickling down his cheeks. Uncle Edvard was stony and red-faced.

I am so proud of David and Henry. Of all the boys in the parade for that matter. But to join the army and go fight a war? As I watched them walk by, my only thought was that this may be the last time I see them alive.

I gave David Great-grandfather's New Testament. He said it would bring him luck. I told him that reading it would bring him strength and peace.

Winter

Tuesday, December 31, 1946

It is 2 A.M. and I am in a pensive mood. Right after church, Dad went to bed saying he has seen in the New Year too many times to count.

Mike and Marilyn insisted I go to the Grange with them. I am not sure why I did; I do not enjoy going to dances alone or with them no matter what. I feel like an extra wheel.

Schultzie asked me to dance, and then he just stood in one place and jumped up and down like a kangaroo. I really should have known better than to accept his invitation. I did not know what to do, so I joined him for a few jumps and then jumped off the dance floor. Someone yelled, "That will teach you to mess with her." He then brought me some punch that had been spiked, and it was more spike than punch.

I was ready to go home.

Sheriff Gearig rescued me with a cup of coffee and some sandwiches. It took me a second to recognize him, as he was not wearing his uniform. We sat and visited for the rest of the evening. He must be quite lonely; he has been a widower for almost a year now and most of his children have left home. I am not sure which is worse—war or cancer. They both take those we love.

I believe he would like to remarry. I hope he can find someone his age.

I am feeling the weight of the year. It has been a year of learning to go through the motions without Mom. It is now fifteen months since she went home. Each milestone, each holiday, each meal, each sunrise, and sunset cause hers and David's absence to echo through the house and our hearts.

Adding to the weight on our shoulders, Uncle Edvard has now joined them.

The year has brought new challenges and joys: a new principal at school, Mrs. B. is continuing to chase Dad, a bumper wheat crop—of 30 bushels an acre; cousins are married; and new babies born.

I resolve to be kind, read the Bible through, and learn to control my temper.

* * * * *

Jacob Stewart
Batavia Veteran's Hospital
E Ward
Batavia, New York
December 31, 1946

Florence Stewart
762 Nicholas Street
#12
NYC, NY

Dearest Mother,

Your kind letter arrived yesterday. As always, it was good to hear from you.

I am doing quite well. I graduated from physical therapy yesterday! The therapist said that I walk as well as I ever will. I do not think I am limping; however, there is a pull in the calf muscle when I walk a distance. We can be thankful the bullet went right through my calf and did not tear it up. I have seen so many where the muscles are destroyed.

There will be a small party on the ward tonight. I think a few of the others have sneaked in some liquor. It will be a hollow party, with so many of us missing our loved ones.

I was thankful and surprised that so many of my fellow patients received visits from their families over the holidays. The soldiers and their families had a difficult time relating at first. All were frightened, but soon many of their hearts melted together.

One of the fellows has lost both his legs, but he continues to laugh and tease. He keeps us all in good humor. When things were tense between the family members, he would tell stories and jokes and get them to laugh. He has been attending my Bible classes.

I am glad you were able to take a few days off over Christmas and rest. It sounds as if you had a pleasant time at the Schroeder's house.

I received a letter from Father Taylor, and he plans on visiting. I am so looking forward to that.

Please rest, with your feet up. I will be home soon.

I remain,

Your loving son,

Jacob

Sunday, January 5, 1947
Name Day celebration for people named Hanna

A cold, snowy day.

Dad and I went to church but left right afterward, as the wind came up during the sermon. I had invited Hannah Nelson and her family for dinner, but they wanted to get home in case this turned into a storm.

While I was talking to Hannah about dinner, Mrs. B. came up, listened, then chimed in, "You don't still celebrate that silly, foreign name day foolishness, do you?"

"Name Day is a wonderful way to celebrate with others that are blessed with the same name," Hannah replied.

Mrs. B's name day is listed as September 2. I will have to do something "foreign" for her. I wonder what she would like.

Hannah had a lovely card for me and a little paperback book of stories from the *"Saturday Evening Post."* I gave her a small dresser scarf that I had tried to make in *Hardanger.* My cutwork embroidery is not as intricate as *Bestemor's.* I wish I had been willing to sit still and learn from Grandmother when I had the chance.

I had a beef roast baking in the oven, and it was done to a turn. Mashed potatoes and turnips, carrots, hot beet salad, and an apple pie filled us up.

Dad did the chores. I had popcorn and cider ready when he got home. Afterward, we listened to the radio, while I did handwork.

It is still windy, but it does not look as if this will turn into much.

Tuesday, February 7, 1947

The wind came up during the night and there was a fair bit of snow when the sun came up. Dad did not think the pickup would make it through the snow, so he walked to the farm. He spent the day there and the wind blew him home just in time for supper. I had *potet suppe* and biscuits.

Friday, February 14, 1947

In today's mail was a huge Valentine for Dad, signed "Guess Who."

The VFW Auxiliary had a basket supper auction. I had so wanted to stay home, but Dad said we should go since the money went for a good cause. Most of the women made up such beautiful baskets, hoping to catch the right man's eye. I did not want anyone to know which basket was mine, so I made up my basket as plain and boring as I could.

One of the first baskets to sell was beautiful with crepe paper roses. Later I saw Toothless Hiram, sitting with that basket, gnawing on cold chicken salad sandwiches. Mrs. B. sat glumly across the table from him.

When my basket came up for auction, Sheriff Gearig was the first to bid, but stopped at $5.00. Melvin Wiese and Mr. Warren bid it up to $15. Everyone must have realized it was mine, since my face was redder than my hair! All the teasing and laughing made it worse. Then some of the men saw what was happening and jumped in, to save me or scare me, I am not sure which. Oh, it caused some good laughs.

Then Uncle Bob and Dad joined in!

In the end, I enjoyed a nice supper with Michael and Marilyn and Dad. Marilyn told me she kicked Mike and made him buy my basket. I cannot believe it went for $35.50! I told Dad they could not afford that, and he should help pay for it. Michael just laughed and said it was for the veterans. He also had to tease Marilyn, since he only paid $8.10 for her basket. With both baskets we had plenty to eat.

When we were getting ready to go, Mrs. Roberts had to come up and say, "Hanna Karlina Morland, your mother would be so ashamed of you, parading yourself like that in front of all these people."

I could only stare at her with my mouth gaping open. I am so glad there is no school tomorrow, so I do not have to face Mrs. B.

Saturday, February 15, 1947

I spent the day cleaning the house and did a few loads of laundry. I cannot believe how much dirt just Dad and I can drag in. I hung most of the laundry outside, and it quickly freeze dried. The dresses and shirts I hung in the basement.

Since we could not celebrate Marilyn's birthday yesterday, I invited them to come for supper. They spent too much time laughing about last night and those men bidding for my basket. She seemed pleased with the table runner I crocheted for her. She is always so busy with her small brood that I also made some cookies for her to take home.

I should not try to clean the house and do laundry all in the same day. I ran out of time to get ready for supper. I was glad I had written down the Forty-Five Minute Pork Chop Dinner and Turnip Salad from last week's *Your Neighbor Lady* radio program. Both turned out to be quite tasty. Marilyn even asked for the recipes.

I made her favorite German Chocolate Cake for dessert.
Dad said he prefers his turnips boiled.

Monday, February 17, 1947

A cold, blustery morning. I wore David's old chore boots with two pair of wool socks. I am sure I looked a sight, but I wanted to arrive at school with warm feet.

I barely got into my room, before Rosanna arrived with a thermos of coffee. Rosanna had started whispering to me about Mrs. B. when she stuck her head in the door.

"They only spent so much for your basket because word got around that you made a sour cream raisin pie from *my* recipe." Then she quickly tippity-tapped down the hall.

Wednesday, February 19, 1947
Ash Wednesday

We did not try to go to church. The wind came up late this afternoon, so we listened to a service on the radio. Dad did book work, and I knitted while we enjoyed Tommy Dorsey and Jack Paar, on the radio.

* * * * *

Bishop Taylor
St. John the Divine
Episcopal Church of America
New York, New York
February 20, 1947

Mrs. Graham Stewart
762 Nicholas Street
#12
NYC, NY

My dear Mrs. Stewart,

Last week, my wife and I made a journey to visit your son, Jacob. I am amiss in not having written to you earlier. I was able to spend two days with him. We discussed many weighty topics. He continues to have a fine, although questioning, mind.

When I arrived, our Jacob was in the day room playing billiards. The atmosphere was cheerful and light, with jazz playing on the radio. There was a double amputee telling stories and making everyone laugh.

Jacob is in good spirits and looking forward to his dismissal. I was not surprised to learn he has been his usual self and has used the time wisely to point many a soul to salvation. He has started several Bible studies and has filled in for the Chaplain.

He told me of his journey from Germany where he was wounded, and then to the evacuation hospital in Belgium, then to England, and finally to the US and the hospital in Batavia. You mentioned, when we last spoke, that neither the Army nor Jacob had related to you how he, a medic, was wounded.

Normally I would leave that to Jacob; however, the extent of his wounds justifies me in breaking confidentiality. I want you to be prepared when he returns home. I am quite surprised his commanding officer has not yet written to you. That is standard procedure.

As you know, he was injured in Germany. The wounded were being cared for in a bomb-damaged church, which was supposed to be quite a distance behind enemy lines. Late one evening the enemy began to bomb that area. The church caught fire, and while the medics were evacuating the soldiers, Jacob sustained third degree burns on his arms, chest, and face. He continued with the evacuation until his commanding officer insisted that he be treated for his own wounds. As he was walking to the people carrier, he was shot, by a sniper, in the left calf. The bullet ripped through the muscle and did not damage any bones.

He continues to question the war, his involvement, and his injuries, and finally the nature and omnipotence of God. However, his belief in God remains intact.

In hindsight, we should <u>not</u> have encouraged him to enlist as a medic instead of as a conscientious objector, where he could have served here at home in relative safety, and he would not have been wounded. Since we cannot turn back the days, we must trust our Almighty Father to lead him to peace.

Through it all, I, myself, am asking all the same questions that Jacob asked us in 1941. I cannot find any answers. I do know and trust a God that cares and abides with us daily. "Thou art good, and doest good; teach me thy statutes." Psalm 119:68. This verse has been a great encouragement to me. I continue to believe that God is good and does good. I trust that can be your strength also.

I will continue to monitor our Jacob's convalescence and relate to you any information to which I am privy.

He misses you and looks forward to his return home so he can provide for you.

Please remember me in your humble prayers.

Sincerely yours,

Bishop P. Taylor

* * * * *

Thursday, February 27, 1947
My Golden Birthday!
27 on the 27ᵗʰ!

Dad surprised me by getting up and making *eggpannekaker* for breakfast. I got out a jar of *bringebærsirup* I had been saving for something special and ate it with relish. Is there a better way to start your day than egg pancakes and raspberry syrup?

At school, when I came in from monitoring last recess, Mrs. Altfillesch and Mrs. Smith were in the classroom with cupcakes and hot chocolate. The children gave me cards and many cherished trinkets.

The person that gave me his heart was Billy Green. He came up with a determined red face and a clenched fist. When he opened it, it contained a small black arrowhead. He offered it to me as a gift, with tears spilling out of his eyes. "I found this by the lake. It's an old Indian arry head. They used it to shoot birds."

I could see he did not want to give it away. With a catch in my voice, I told him, "Billy you know how I am now old and forgetful and lose things. Would you please keep it safe for me? I will need to look at it now and then because it is so beautiful."

"Oh, yes Miz Morland!"

Mrs. Gehm called the school and asked me to stop on my way home. She had sewn a yellow gingham apron with chicken scratches for me. I wanted to stay for tea, but she shooed me on my way.

As I walked into the house, The Girls greeted me with a table set with cake, coffee, and a pile of gifts. I received a few knickknacks and dishes and the *1946*

Your Neighbor Lady Cookbook. After everyone left, Marilyn gave me a new journal and a piece of blue wool. She wants me to come over on Saturday, so we can sew together. She really likes her new electric machine.

Since we graduated from high school, The Girls do not get together as often. I had not seen Carol's new baby until today.

In the mail, I received a flowery birthday card. It was signed, *From your friend, Mel.* Dad saw it but did not comment. Later when I added it to the fire in the stove, he said that was the best use for it.

Saturday, March 1, 1947

I spent the day sewing at Marilyn's house. We took turns using her electric machine. I cannot believe how slick it worked. I wondered if I saved the egg money how long it would be before I could afford one.

Mike and the boys cleared out and said they would eat at the Ritz Café with Dad.

The rest of The Girls were there for dinner and brought their sewing or hand work.

We listened to *Your Neighbor Lady* and ate a light snack before they all went home. It was a hen party, but I enjoyed it, nevertheless.

Sunday, March 2, 1947
Name Day celebration for people named Ernsts

It is nice that Dad's and my *Navnedag* both fell on Sunday this year.

Dad did chores early, and I had Ernest Reimer and Ernst Martin and their families for the evening. The men talked farming while they cranked a freezer of ice cream; the ladies gossiped, and I played cards with the children. I served popcorn, Mom's Yellow Layer Cake, and ice cream.

I think that Dad and the other Ernsts enjoyed being together on their day.

Friday, March 7, 1947

A cold, clear morning. Aunt Julia and Uncle Herb arrived on the morning train. I had coffee and *skolebrød* ready for them. While we were eating, Aunt Julia leaned into the table and whispered, "Have you heard how he died?"

I was not kind. I leaned into the table and replied as conspiratorially as I could, "I talked to Myrna last week at church and she said he had taken to ailing." Dad gave me a look that told me I should have known better.

"Taken to ailing. Hmmm, I wonder what she meant by that."

"Good grief Julia, Hendrick was 87. He probably died of old age," Uncle Herb chided her.

"You never know what could have happened, Myrna is divorced."

Now it was Dad's turn to try to detour her. "Being divorced does not make her a murderer."

"Who said she murdered Mr. Norgaard? She is divorced, and you never know what can happen. I will ask Ina."

She then asked about Henry. "Have the Norgaards heard from the Army about Henry? Do they know if he is alive or dead?"

"No, it has been almost three years and they have had no word from the Army," Dad told her.

"I wonder how the Army can just lose a body. You would think they could keep better track of things." I could not believe she said that. With all the death and destruction, how could they keep everything straight?

The funeral was pleasant, with our remembering the life of one of the area's pioneers. I was glad that Henry and David were only mentioned in hushed tones, that way we could focus on Mr. Norgaard and his life, not on our suffering.

Afterwards, Myrna and Dad sat and compared stories. I knew that the Norgaards came on the same ship as my grandparents, but I did not know they were also from Grimstad. That makes our connection much stronger, knowing it goes all the way back to the same village in Norway. I was also amazed to learn how many Bible verses Mr. Norgaard had committed to memory, both in Norwegian and English.

Aunt Julia and Ina Roberts had their heads together at the funeral.

We were invited to the Ostegaard's for supper.

Sunday, March 9, 1947

Aunt Julia and Uncle Herb left for Canton on the late train. The house is quiet now and I like it that way.

Tuesday, March 11, 1947

We awoke to a heavy snowfall. Before breakfast was over the wind was roaring. Dad took me to school in the model A Ford. I'm glad it still has on the chains from the last storm.

Only about half of my class came. Right at nine, Mr. Warren told "us" that school was dismissed and that "we" should send "our" students home. "We" bundled up. I had my first graders in line at the front doors to pair them with an older brother or sister, or neighbor. The Green family refused to leave without me. Mr. Warren shooed them out the door, but they waited outside for me. He opened the door and yelled against the wind, "WE must go home."

When he left, I let them back in and hurriedly got ready for the walk home. Billy took my hand and told me he would make "darn sure" I made it home. He even walked me up to the door.

Dad must have stayed at the farm. We do need to get that phone hooked up again.

Wednesday, March 12, 1947

Still the blizzard rages.

I used this long day to worry about Dad and get some much-needed mending done. I also sewed a small book cover for Aunt Julia, which I will mail later. I will not send her a Name Day greeting since she does not like her name and insists on being called Julia. Dad says Uncle Herb will have the final say. He has already ordered their tombstone and had Ellinor engraved on it.

I cleaned out the closet in the guest room and dusted all the bookshelves. Since Dad wasn't home, I didn't cook proper meals, I just snacked.

Thursday, March 13, 1947

Day three. This storm will surely wear itself out soon. More worrying, and sewing, and cleaning, and baking, and worrying.

Friday, March 14, 1947

At noon, the wind died down, and the sun came out. Dad arrived home in time for supper. I ran and clung to him like a little girl. It was so good to have him home. He wonders if we should move to the farm for the rest of the winter. With Uncle Edvard gone, it is hard to drive back and forth to do chores. He said he would keep the chains on the pickup, and I could drive back and forth to school.

I made some thick chicken noodle soup and had sourdough biscuits for supper. For dessert, I offered apple pie, chocolate cake, cinnamon rolls, and gingersnaps. I told him that all the baking was a result of all my worrying.

I know that once he is at the farm, he is fine. I just worry that he may be stuck somewhere in between. I am glad Toothless Hiram watches to make certain he goes by.

Saturday, March 15, 1947

It was 58 years ago today that my grandparents arrived in De Smet, from Norway, and bought the relinquishment. I think I would never have been brave enough to leave all that was familiar and move so far from home. The pine trees that *Bestemor* started from seeds she brought with her still stand in a circle around the house.

I loved sitting with *Bestemor* and *Bestefar* listening to them tell stories of the early years.

Dawn was cold and clear, a most welcome relief from the storm. I went to school and tidied up and got ready for next week.

Wednesday, March 19, 1947

Today was one of those days I was so thankful I am a teacher. Something in Billy Green's head clicked. He realized he could read and took off. His hug and praise telling me *I am the best teacher in the whole wide world* have made it all worthwhile.

Friday, March 21, 1947

After school, I walked the mile to the farm.

Today, Dad culled all the old hens. He had them dressed and cooling in the cellar. He offered to stay home tomorrow, and help with canning, but Aunt Doris called and offered to help, getting him off the hook. Supper was macaroni and cheese, black-eyed peas, and cooked cabbage.

Louise called and said she and Stanley signed papers for the old Hansen farm.

Saturday, March 22, 1947

Aunt Doris arrived right after breakfast and helped me cut up the chickens. I did canner after canner full, with the windows wide open. The smell of meat canning filled the house. My hair smells of it. I cannot stand the smell of meat canning.

I will have 42 quarts of chicken in the cellar plus I gave Aunt Doris 8 quarts for all her help. She hardly wanted to take that many. However, I told her if she did not, I would take them to her house, and put them in her cellar anyway.

I got the mess cleaned up and am ready for a bath. The clock just struck eleven.

Wednesday, March 26, 1947

With it being warmer yesterday and today, the playground is a soupy lake. During afternoon recess, Mrs. B. brought Billy Green in by the ear. He was soaking wet, shivering, and his lips were blue. I quickly wrapped him up in my coat and carried him downstairs. Rosanna helped me strip him down. We wrapped a blanket around him and set him by the open oven to warm up. I sent his brother, Ben, home for dry clothes.

Billy enjoyed his time in the kitchen and was not happy to return to the classroom. He bragged how Rosanna had given him hot cocoa and toast with jam.

Thursday, March 27, 1947

Another storm blew up during the night. Dad spent the night at the farm. He thought this was going to happen and made plans to stay there. I worry less knowing he is safe.

Toothless Hiram is helping with the lambing. Dad offered that he could sleep in the house, but he insisted on setting up camp in the *sauefjøs*. Toothless Hiram said the sheep barn is as comfortable as any house.

I am glad we sold most of the ewes last autumn and have only twenty left to lamb out. It was far too much work without Uncle Edvard, although, I would have missed the little lambs if we did not have a few. We have very few bottle lambs this year.

Although I am safe in town, this house seems so big and rambling when I am alone in it.

I spent most of the day in the kitchen with the stove door open and my feet propped on it reading next month's book for the De Smet Ladies' Book Club, *Mrs. Mike,* by Benedict and Nancy Freeman. I need to pass it on to Mrs. Moody as soon as this storm quits. It took me a bit to get into it, but it is good.

Saturday, March 29, 1947

I was ready to get out, so I walked to the post office to get the mail. Mrs. Roberts was there. She wondered if I shouldn't be home cleaning house instead of walking to the post office.

It was not until I was almost home that it occurred to me that Mrs. Roberts was at the post office too and not home cleaning house. I began to wonder if she has any dust kittens under her beds. What evil lurks under her beds? Only the Shadow knows.

Sunday, March 30, 1947

Dad dropped me off at church while he went out to chore. The streets are still full of snow. But with David's chore boots and two pair of wool socks I made it nicely home through the snow. Mrs. Roberts gave me an odd look, but I cannot walk through snow in pumps.

In the afternoon, Dad wrote letters, and I sewed on my Magic Vine quilt. Mom started appliqueing this quilt when I was still in school. She was almost done when David died, and then she put it away.

It was a pleasant and sad time as I continued where she left off. Her neat, even stitches contrast with my clumsy ones. I am glad she had all the pieces cut, so all I need to do is finish sewing it together. Dad and I reminisced about the fabric and from which dress or shirt each one was created. One piece of fabric was from a shirt she sewed for David to wear on his first date with Clara. We laughed about how the A ran out of gas and they had to walk home. Later we found out that Schultzie had drained the tank.

We do not talk about them much. It was good to remember the good times. The happy times before the war.

For dinner, I put in a roast, carrots, onions, and potatoes. I used some of the canned peaches for pie. Good smells filled the house.

Spring

Tuesday, April 1, 1947

Mrs. B. came into my room today, and said, "I love your father, and I am going to marry him. April Fools!"

She is not fooling anyone but herself.

When I told Dad, he only gritted his teeth and rolled his eyes.

I told him I was glad Toothless Hiram was helping him with the lambing.

"I wish you would not call him that. He has a name. He has been a good neighbor and friend. He has a kind heart and would help anyone that is in need. Even if he did not do that, he deserves to be called by his right name. I have never understood why people treat him as if he is a joke." Dad's reproof really stings. I always knew he did not like that name. I should have been more careful.

I apologized and will try to never say it again.

Wednesday, April 2, 1947

I felt out of sorts all day from last night's reproof.

Dad worked on getting the drill ready. He thinks it is going to warm up and dry up soon. He is anxious to get his spring wheat in. It is always a worry whether we will get a crop or not.

I am so looking forward to spring greens. I fried the last of the potatoes tonight. Good old Dad did not say anything about fried pork chops, fried potatoes, and chocolate pudding.

Uncle Bob and Aunt Doris came over for the evening. She helped me cut and sew rag strips for Peggy.

Before devotions, Dad apologized for being so harsh. With his eyes twinkling he said, "Besides when Hiram yawns you can count up to five teeth." I hope I learned a lesson on how to treat people.

Thursday, April 3, 1947
Maundy Thursday

Mr. Warren came in today and did not say a word to any of us. He just stood and stared and then walked out. I will never understand that man if I live to be a 100.

We went to church for Maundy Thursday services. I wore the blue wool dress made from the fabric Marilyn gave me. Mrs. Green told me it brings out the blue of my eyes.

There was a raw wind, so I also wore Mom's light blue sweater. Mrs. Roberts must have recognized it because she came sniffing around as if she had something to say. I just looked at her and waited. The service of forgiveness must have won her over for a few minutes, as she had nothing to say.

Dad suffered through hamburger gravy and biscuits.

Dad is done lambing. The last ewe came through with triplets today, all ewe lambs.

Friday, April 4, 1947
Good Friday

Oh my… I was in the lunchroom, and Mrs. B. came up and said, "Honey, I heard that the principal was in your room yesterday and gave you a talking to. I'm so sorry. I am sure you will make a good teacher with more practice."

I just smiled and asked her if her class was learning their multiplication tables. Her smile slipped off her face, she squinted her eyes at me, and her heels tippity-tapped away.

Our school was out early for Good Friday services. I walked to church with a gaggle of children following me. Every time I turned, they would giggle, run, and hide.

It felt comforting to slip into our pew next to Dad. The somber hymns and weather seemed to fit my mood.

For supper, we were comforted with *fruktsuppe* and *fritert brød*. Although, I do not think that it was as good as when Mom made it.

Saturday, April 5, 1947

Papers to grade, house to clean, garden seeds to sort, bread to bake, and laundry to do. What did I do? I curled up on the sofa and read. There was a brisk north wind, and I did not want to do anything.

I did rouse myself enough to bake three loaves of pumpkin bread and take one loaf to Mrs. Gehm. Her "'tism" is really bothering her in this cold. I admire her outlook on life. She remains happy despite all that comes her way.

I also left a loaf in Hiram's mailbox.

Then I quickly picked up the house and called Mrs. Callahan to see if she would help me with the laundry next week. I feel guilty about spending money when I can do the work. She said she would help me.

Sunday, April 6, 1947
Easter!

Easter Sunday dawned cold and clear. A heavy frost covered everything.

The pullets are laying so we had three pullet eggs apiece.

I played for both Sunday School and the church service. My heart soared with the hymn, "I Know That My Redeemer Lives" only reminding me we have sung it far too recently at funerals.

After church, Mrs. Roberts came up and told me that a lady would never go into "Toothless Hiram's" house. I told her that I had never been in Hiram's house.

"That's not what I heard." All I could do was sigh.

We invited the Larsens and the Mc Kinneys for dinner. I was a bit embarrassed at the house and the dust, however, neither woman mentioned it. To help with dinner, Mrs. Mc Kinney brought canned apricot pie and pickles, and Mrs. Larsen brought a jar of beans and two loaves of bread.

I got a ham at Peschl's. It looked like a good one, but it was a challenge to chew. There is a lot left over for next week.

After dinner, the children and I dyed eggs. They got more dye on the floor than their eggs, but they each left with a nice basket full.

Monday, April 7, 1947
Easter Monday

Today I cleaned the house and did laundry, making up for being so lazy on Saturday. Mrs. Callahan spent the morning with me. Before I could stop her, she used the rinse water and washed the kitchen floor. Moreover, after all that, Mrs. Callahan refused payment. Her parting words were that she was only repaying Mom for all her kindnesses.

I got all my grading done and am ready for another week of school.

I used the leftover ham for scalloped potatoes and ham.

Tuesday, April 8, 1947

It is bedtime, and I cannot remember much about the day. I went to school and came home. I am tired.

More ham today. This time I put it in bean soup.

Wednesday, April 9, 1947

It was cool and drippy all day. We could not go out for recess, so the children were restless. I read in the paper that there were tornadoes in Texas, Oklahoma, and Kansas, 181were killed and 970 injured.

In the evening, I finished sewing all the strips I had for Peggy.

For supper, I fried some canned chicken, and we ate it with boiled potatoes and gravy.

* * * * *

Jacob Stewart
Batavia Veteran's' Hospital
E Ward
Batavia, NY
April 10, 1947

Mrs. Graham Stewart
762 Nicholas Street
NYC, NY

Dearest Mother,

I will be arriving home on the 12th. It will be so good to see you. The doctor says my wounds have sufficiently healed so I can return home. You will not recognize me with the beard I have grown. I wanted to cover the scars.

Please do not come to meet me at the station. It is too far for you to walk. I will come to the flat and spend many days resting and enjoying your good cooking.

I plan to find work. I am not sure what is available as there are so many other returning servicemen who are looking for work.

God will provide. I can even follow Father's footsteps and work on the docks.

Your loving son,
Jacob

* * * * *

Friday, April 11, 1947

It was dry enough for Dad to put in a full day of planting. I took supper to the farm.

I am going to have to get out there soon and clean. The house is a mess!

We had porcupine meatballs, green beans, carrot-raisin salad, and some doughnuts that Rosanna gave me.

Saturday, April 12, 1947

Dad was in the field all day. I cleaned the house and did a bit of laundry.

Sunday, April 13, 1947

The church reorganization and building came up this morning at church. It is hard for Dad; with this talk of joining the two country churches and then tearing all three down and building another. Our family has been members of this church since it was founded. He has not said much, but he is unhappy with all the talk. It seems to involve money, men's egos, and the declining membership of the country churches.

After church and dinner, we rested and read.

Marilyn called and invited us for supper. Her home is always so lively. The men talked farming, and we gossiped. Shelly is in Mrs. B.'s class this year and having such a struggle. When the children could not hear, we laughed again at all the tricks the boys played on Mrs. B. With our sides aching we remembered how she gave us all lice.

Monday, April 14, 1947
Navnedag celebration for people named Ellinor

I got to school early to get ready for class. I smelled smoke coming from the girls' restroom. Going in to investigate, I found Mrs. B was in the stall with her dress hiked up and her garters hanging, leaning forward with her elbows resting on her knees, and smoking. What a sight! Her nylons had fallen around her ankles. I just mumbled, "Good morning" and left.

Later, after lunch, she came up to me and said she had found that burning cigarette and was merely picking it up to get rid of it. Then she said, "Can you believe someone would leave a burning cigarette in the restroom?"

"My dad thinks smoking is a disgusting habit."

"He does? Ah uh, it is a good thing I do not smoke," she quickly replied.

I wonder, if she does not smoke, why she smells like cigarette smoke all the time.

It was quite cold and windy today. It seems as if spring will never come. The crocuses are peeping up on the south side of the house. I hope to go out on the butte this weekend and see if I can find some Pasque flowers.

Dad told me that until the dusty days our south pasture was full of Pasque flowers.

I made sweet potato and sausage pie for supper. I have one sweet potato left and have started sprouting it. It is a bit late but as cold as it is, I doubt I will be able to plant the sprouts before the end of May.

* * * * *

April 17, 1947
Bishop Paul Taylor
St. John the Divine
Episcopal Church of America
NYC, NY

Jacob Stewart
762 Nicholas Street
#12
NYC, NY

Dear Jacob Stewart,

Greetings in the name of our risen Lord Jesus.

This letter is to inform you that you have been placed as the parish priest at St. Stephen's Episcopalian Parish in De Smet, South Dakota.

The placement committee has been in contact with Bishop Bradbury in Sioux Falls, South Dakota. They and I believe your skills will be best used in a smaller congregation.

The South Dakota diocese has not been able to place a priest at St. Stephen's since before the war. I believe you will find a congregation who will respond well to you. Your first order of business will be to make visitations and start having services as soon as possible.

Please alert Bishop Bradbury as to your arrival and he will further direct you.

Sincerely,

Bishop Taylor

P. S. My dear Jacob, I continue to pray for your healing. My wife and I will watch over your mother until you are able to send for her. Please find enclosed $100 for your travel expenses. I know you will have a difficult time accepting it. You may consider it a loan if that is easier. Godspeed, my son.

* * * * *

Thursday, April 24, 1947

Willa Cather, one of my favorite authors, died today. America lost one of its best authors.

* * * * *

April 29, 1947
Knox, Pennsylvania

Mother,
    I am sitting on the steps of the post office and once again overcome with emotion as I remember your kindness and generosity. When my trunk arrives in Dakota, I will be the best-dressed vicar in the state. I wonder how many hours of extra work you took on to afford such a fine suit.
    I am looking forward to being settled in so you can join me and become a lady of leisure at the vicarage.

I remain,
Your loving son,
Jacob

Mrs. G. Stewart
765 Nicholas Street
#12
NYC, NY

* * * * *

May 6, 1947
Van Wert, Ohio

Mother,
Traveling has been slow. I punctured a tire and had to walk quite a distance. Pushing a motorcycle with a flat tire is hard work. A farmer finally took pity on me and gave me a ride. He liked to sing, and we sang several hymns to-gether. The sun has been warm and pleasant after a few days of clouds and rain. I spent last night in a barn with some other former soldiers. They had such different stories to tell. I could only re-main silent, as I reflected on my own experience.
Do not work too hard. Promise me you will rest.

I remain,
Your loving son,
Jacob

Mrs. G. Stewart
762 Nicholas St.
#12
NYC, NY

* * * * *

Wednesday, May 7, 1947

It was unseasonably warm today, making our classroom unbearable. So, we took our books out and settled under the largest elm to read. Mr. Warren came and said, "We cannot learn if we are sitting under a tree reading. We need to remain in our classroom." My class and I lumbered back into our classroom.

For supper, Dad brought some asparagus and rhubarb in from the farm. We had creamed asparagus on toast, and I made a pie.

Thursday, May 8, 1947

Again, it was hot. So, we returned to our tree, and we took our books and notebooks. The children recorded the number of bird songs and other sounds they heard.

Mr. Warren came to us and said, "Miss Morland, we talked to us yesterday and told us that we are not to be reading outside. Learning is to take place in our classroom."

I smiled as sweetly as I could and said, "Mr. Warren, when someone uses first person plural, it includes themselves. You said 'we' could not read. You were not with 'us,' and I am not reading, so I thought *they* could read. They are not only reading but recording bird songs and any new sounds they hear."

He turned to Billy Green and asked, "What sounds did we hear?"

Billy ever-so-innocently replied, "I do not know what you heard, sir, but I heard a wren, a song sparrow, and Mrs. Penny hollering at Mr. Penny."

Abruptly, Mr. Warren turned on his heel and went inside.

Later he came to me and said, "Mrs. Penny hollering at Mr. Penny hardly constitutes a new sound."

Dad brought in some fresh lamb's quarters, and I had some radishes ready in my garden. They made a tasty spring salad.

Two years ago, today Germany surrendered. So much-and not enough-has happened in the last two years. I would have thought life would return to normal by now.

* * * * *

Somewhere in Iowa
May 8, 1947

Dear Mother,
   I did want to send you a postcard today to let you know I have made it to western Iowa, but where I am, I am not quite sure. I will post this at the next town I am in. The weather has been favorable, and I have been able to exchange work for food or lodging. I believe I shall make it to South Dakota soon.
   I will send another postcard when I can.
          I remain,
          Your loving son,
               Jacob
P. S. I mailed this in Orange City, Iowa

Florence Stewart
762 Nicholas St.
#12
NYC, NY

* * * * *

Friday, May 9, 1947

Our heat is over, and today we shivered. It was cold and cloudy all morning and then, as the children were returning from dinner, it poured. The classroom smelled of wet woolens and steamy children. I sent a note to the office and asked Irene to call Dad and ask him to bring milk and the ingredients for hot chocolate. He arrived in his overalls smelling of the barnyard. Rosanna gladly stirred up the hot chocolate for us.

Mr. Warren again visited with me." Miss Morland, how often must we be reminded that our job is to teach. We should not be making special requests of the cooks."

Mrs. B. later told me I should not worry. The children needed something warm to drink. I wonder how she hears about everything, sometimes, it seems, even before it even happens.

Today as I walked past St. Stephen's Episcopal Church, a man arrived on a motorcycle. He took off his leather helmet and stood there staring at the church. I said hello. He was so distracted he did not reply for a bit.

Creamed asparagus over toast warmed us up nicely.

Saturday, May 10, 1947

Household and gardening chores filled my day.

Marilyn was in town shopping and stopped in for a cup of tea.

I opened a jar of chicken, added rice, and the last of last year's carrots and made a nice, thick soup.

Sunday, May 11, 1947

Spring has again returned; it was such a soft, warm day. After church and dinner, I went with Dad to the farm. As I walked in the south pasture, I picked a beautiful bouquet of spring wildflowers.

When we arrived home, the man that I saw in front of St. Stephen's was sitting on our porch. Dad turned to me and said, "Oh, yes, this is the new vicar; I invited him to supper." Oh my! I scurried around and made supper. I opened a jar of sausage and boiled some potatoes; fresh asparagus, canned tomatoes, and peaches filled us up.

It was not a company supper, but I think he liked it. He ate enough! As we walked him to the door, he apologized for eating so much. Then he confessed he was out of money, and this was the first meal he had eaten in two days. He does not know when he will get paid; the bishop has not contacted him. He asked if there was any other work available for him.

Dad told him he should take his meals with us until he gets paid. So, it looks as if I will be cooking for three for a while.

Monday, May 12, 1947

Promptly at 6 A.M., the new vicar arrived for breakfast. I thought, after last night's supper, he would have been filled up. However, he ate six slices of bacon and three eggs. I lost count of the pieces of toast. That was what I had fixed for the three of us. I quickly fried more for Dad and me. The vicar sat back and enjoyed his coffee.

Dad reached for the Bible for morning devotions. He read his customary Psalm and a selection from the New Testament, and then we knelt to pray.

After we stood up and I started to clear the table, the vicar just stood there and looked as if he had something to say but said nothing. He wished us a good day and left.

The school day was quite typical.

The birds called to us; the insects buzzed in and out of the room, making us restless. They begged us to explore the prairie.

Dad said the vicar came promptly at noon. He was covered with dust as he had been cleaning the church. And Dad said he was quiet.

After school, I had a nice long walk west on the road to Manchester; some flags were blooming at the edge of the slough. I got my shoes muddy picking them. The bright, blue wild irises are a cheerful addition to the kitchen table.

I was in the kitchen preparing supper when I felt someone in the room. Turning, I saw the vicar standing in the doorway. He did not say anything. He was staring at the flags. Quietly as if to himself or someone else, as if I were not present, he started talking about a family in Holland that had iris growing along the dike and that they had to eat the bulbs during the war. They saved one and hoped that once again they would have flags growing along the dike.

Then he turned to me and asked if I thought the flowers had returned.

Not knowing what to say, I opened and shut my mouth a few times but said nothing.

Dad walked in and saved me.

During supper, the vicar was distracted and stared at the flags. Before he left, he asked where I had picked them and if he could pick some. Dad offered to take him tomorrow. Then Dad got his coat and walked the vicar home.

I stood on the porch and watched them, wondering what all he had seen in the war.

It is late. Dad has still not gotten home.

Tuesday, May 13, 1947

I was in bed when I heard Dad come in. I got up and asked him why he was so late. Dad just said he and the vicar had sat on the church steps and talked too long. His hug was stronger than usual, as he bid me good night. I wondered what he had heard and if his own wounds would be reopened.

I sometimes look at my life and how the deaths of Mom, David, and Uncle Edvard have brought an end to my future. I dwell on what is no longer and cannot think of what the future may be. Will we ever be able to leave this behind?

On a brighter note, Mr. Warren breezed in and out during spelling, without saying a word; I was sure he would come back later. Of course, I was right. He came in after I returned from front door duty." Miss Morland, do we actually think drawing pictures when we are scheduled to be learning spelling words is appropriate?"

"Ahh, Mr. Warren, my students were learning their spelling words as they drew pictures. They were hiding the words in the picture."

"We did not see any hidden words."

I handed him some of the pictures, and he stood and stared at them for a few moments. Then as he laid them on the desk, he said, "Writing our words ten times would better inscribe them in our brains." Pointing to one of the pictures, he continued, "We have hidden the word bush in this bush and the word bird in this bird. We must continue to learn our spelling words in the proper fashion. If such a trend continues, we may be learning our words in a crossword puzzle." He turned on his heel and left.

I am often surprised at the wisdom of that man. I liked the suggestion of the crossword puzzle so much that I quickly made one on the blackboard with a list of clues for tomorrow's spelling lesson.

The vicar remains quiet. We hardly know him, but it seems a fog has settled over him and he is distracted.

* * * * *

May 13, 1947
De Smet, South Dakota

Mother,
I have arrived. I had wanted to let you know sooner but could not afford a postcard. Just today, I found 2 pennies lying on the road. God provides. De Smet is a friendly town, and we will be most happy here. I have spent some time walking around looking for a small house to rent. The church has not been used in many years, so I spend most of my time cleaning and doing minor repairs.
Saturday, as I sat on the steps, a man walked up and warmly greeted me. Under his beard is a genuine smile and above are kind blue eyes. He invited me to dinner.
I will write a letter soon,
Jacob

Mrs. Graham Stewart
762 Nicholas St.
NYC, NY

* * * * *

Wednesday, May 14, 1947

What do you know! We started the day with the spelling crossword, and guess who walked into the classroom? "Are we doing crossword puzzles?"

"Yes, the children are, thank you for the fun idea. They are excited about it."

The vicar was less pensive and more talkative today. Dad put aside corn planting and spent the day with him and helped him clean the church. His little congregation must be glad to have a regular minister again. The church has been closed for so long; I think since the war began. I wonder how many people will come back.

Thursday, May 15, 1947

The school day was uneventful. I did not see Mr. Warren all day. I certainly hope he is avoiding me.

As I walked into the house, the phone was ringing. It was Mrs. Roberts calling to "remind" me that since Mrs. Gates cannot have the De Smet Ladies Book Club this month that I needed to host it. My Jammers! I almost swore at her. Then I remembered to live above such minor irritations. So, Saturday afternoon, I will serve tea to a house full of ladies. I have no idea what to serve!

It is too early for strawberries, and some will consider dried apple or rhubarb pie too ordinary.

At supper, I told Dad about the De Smet Ladies' Book Club. He just looked at the vicar and started laughing.

There was fresh lettuce sprinkled with vinegar for supper. I could make a complete meal of lettuce in the spring. Contrarily, the men need more, therefore, I fried some potatoes and ground beef patties.

Friday, May 16, 1947

Your Neighbor Lady came to my rescue! Today Wynn featured a recipe for rhubarb crisp. It was effortless and sounded so tasty. I immediately made some for supper. Served warm with a small amount of cream poured over it was delicious. I shall make two pans for tomorrow's meeting of the De Smet Ladies' Book Club.

The rhubarb crisp, bread and butter, cold roast beef, and baked beans were supper enough with all the cleaning I needed to do.

Dad just sighed when I lamented about hosting the De Smet Ladies' Book Club. He reminded me that I did not need to be a member, and it is only every few years that I must serve as hostess and that when Mom went home, Mrs. Roberts was the first one here with food.

"Only so she could be the first to hear all the news and spread it!" I retorted. I then got the look that said, "be more accepting and give others a chance." I chose to ignore the look and scurried to clean the house.

Dad explained to the perplexed vicar that my grandmother had been a member and mother had endured it; and even though I am, not yet (NOT YET!), considered an old biddy, I was an honorary member.

One part of me is pleased, and maybe a bit honored, to be part of a group of women that have been part of our family for three generations. The other part is irritated at their gossiping, feelings of superiority and entitlement, and lack of depth of thought.

Looking at them as a group, it is really Mrs. Roberts and her small band of biddies that would have such feelings and inflict them on others. The other women have reared families and help their husbands in the business or farm. Solid people.

Saturday, May 17, 1947

I had the rhubarb picked and in the sink by the time the vicar arrived for breakfast. Dad told him it would be best if they cleared out right away and made room for all the biddies.

I tried to give him a look that said, "be more accepting and give others a chance," but he just laughed at me and left for the farm, telling the vicar, on the way out that they would eat at the diner, and he should meet him there at noon.

The vicar finished his coffee and began cleaning the rhubarb. He stayed and helped me get ready. He did not have a lot to say but seemed to know what needed to be done and did an excellent job. Then, while I made the rhubarb crisp, he washed dishes and swept the kitchen floor.

Promptly at 2 o'clock, the members of the De Smet Ladies' Book Club arrived. All my anger and feelings melted away as I greeted the women that supported Mom and have been so much a part of my life.

After settling down in Mom's rocker, Mrs. Roberts asked if my vacuum sweeper was broken. When I ignored her, she then asked me if I needed to bring chairs in from the farmhouse so that I had enough. I told her I had another one in the kitchen if she would like to switch.

After our business meeting, we began to discuss *Pavilion of Women,* by Pearl S. Buck. It was evident some had not been able to read it. The copy from the library had been passed around. I wondered at the wisdom of selecting such a new and expensive book. It cost $1.00.

I served the luncheon on Mom's china snack plates. With each clinking of a fork or cup, I feared a new chip. Then I remembered how Mom loved using her nice things.

The ladies only made polite sounds about the refreshments.

Mrs. Roberts asked if I were still rationing sugar as this rhubarb crisp, "although most delicious was just a mite tart."

She then turned to her neighbor and asked loudly about that "vagabond preacher" that has been seen about town. Who would ever go to his church? And that beard! Does he ever change his clothes? Why is he so quiet and why does he slink around? When no one answered, she turned to me. "You have been seeing a lot of him, have you not?"

"You know Dad, he is always picking up all sorts of strays," I answered, trying to make a joke of it. She responded with a pinched mouth and looked knowingly down her nose at me. She had to leave shortly after that. Her entourage, Mrs. Gable, and Mrs. Penny went with her.

Mrs. B. said, "Honey, she is so mean she must live on sour pickles. I do not care what she says, your dessert, or whatever you happen to call it, was tasty; very, very sour but tasty. I am sure you will be as good a cook as your mother someday." She then got her coat and just before she left, she turned and said, "Ernst does seem to get skinnier all the time. Maybe he could use some good home cooking."

My dad does not look skinny!

With a collective sigh, the ladies smiled and leaned their heads together. Aunt Doris removed her shoes, stretched her legs, and wriggled her toes. Mrs. Williams took off her hat and fanned herself. My dessert was exclaimed over, and they asked for the recipe. We all shared our latest recipe from *Your Neighbor Lady.*

Mrs. Wagner had not seen the vicar, so the ladies described him, using all sorts of words, tall, handsome, bearded, lonely, quiet, thin, stout, friendly, and dark. The only words they all could agree on were tall and handsome.

Mrs. Williams stayed to help clean up. The vicar also arrived and immediately began to wash dishes. She came into the kitchen, with a tray of dishes, and said, "So vagabonds know how to wash dishes." The vicar looked quizzically at me and continued his task. Of course, no one can remain sober with Mrs. Williams around. She began a tale of Dan getting stuck in the laundry chute. Dan had wanted to race his brothers to the basement and decided to use the laundry chute. The vicar has a deep laugh that echoed through the room. It was good to hear him laugh. When he smiles, his eyes crinkle at the corners. He is tall and handsome.

Dad decided we needed to go out for supper, so he took us to the Ritz Café. I enjoyed having supper served to me.

As we walked past St. Stephan's, the vicar told us that tomorrow he planned to have the first service, and would we like to join him? Of course, Dad said we would join him.

Sunday, May 18, 1947

We arrived at 9 A.M. at St. Stephen's. The Gates and the Allens also came.

It was a simple service using their *Book of Common Prayer.* We sang Matins; it was not too unlike our Matins service, so Dad and I were able to follow along. The vicar sang with a clear, steady voice. The Gates and Allens knew the service, so they did better.

We sang without the organ. There is a hole in the bellows. Once it is repaired, it will need to be cleaned and tuned.

The vicar was wearing a worn suit that had obviously been sponged; instead of one of the usual two sets of clothing he had worn since arriving.

After dinner, Dad sat at the table and drank his tea, while the vicar helped with the dishes. I told him I did not want to be bold, but I wondered where he was staying and if he needed any help that I could supply? The vicar said he was sleeping in the church basement and that his trunk was at the station but would need to wait until the diocese sent his check before he picked it up. He washed his clothes in a bucket and hung them up to dry at night. He told me this very matter-of-factly and almost cheerily. He went on to say that his mother had worked many extra hours to buy him a new suit and that it was in the trunk, as was his clerical garb. He was looking forward to getting it, as it also had all his books. One could have almost called him talkative.

The vicar told of being discouraged because he was unable to send his mother a postcard to let her know he had arrived. He had prayed about it and went for a walk and while out walking, he found two pennies.

"But surely you had money when you left New York?" I blurted out. Dad shot me a folded-up forehead look, which the vicar also saw.

"No, Ernst, that is fine. A family friend loaned me $100 for the trip. The second night out I met up with some people that needed the money more than I did. I worked my way out here. The Indian does not use much gas, and often I swept the station or did something to buy a gallon of gas. I would help with farm work for a meal and a place in the barn to sleep. It worked out just fine. God has taken good care of me."

Dad got up and got some paper, envelopes, stamps, and a pen. He apologized for not thinking of it sooner, telling him to please write to his mother. The vicar then settled on the back porch and spent several hours writing. He would pause between thoughts as if he were thinking of just the correct wording. Later, I took him a cup of tea. Of course, I did not look, but just happened to notice his handwriting was precise with each letter formed correctly.

The hens are laying quite well. I fried eggs for sandwiches, using the last of last year's sweet pickles. We seem to be eating more bread than I can keep up with so I will have to buy some tomorrow after school. That means biscuits for breakfast.

* * * * *

May 18, 1947
General Delivery
De Smet, South Dakota

Dearest Mother,

I must first apologize for not writing sooner; I hope you received a postcard from me, announcing my arrival.

I arrived on May 10. De Smet is a clean town and filled with friendly people.

When I arrived at the church, it was evident it had not been used for some time. It is badly in need of paint. The walls seem stout and will stand for a long time. I was looking up at the church and praying for the grace to be a good leader when a young woman came walking down the sidewalk. I was too overcome by emotion to speak. But I must confess not so overwhelmed that I did notice her beauty.

As I said, the church is stout, and the walls are true. With a coat of paint, it will again be an appealing building. It has an elegant, yet solemn, sanctuary with stained glass windows and dark oak furniture. The reredos is dark oak, but the tapestries in it are torn by a sparrow that came in the broken window and made her home in the tapestries and mice built a nest in the organ bellows.

There is a parish hall and basement. For the time being, I have been living in the basement, it is warm and dry. It has a cistern filled from the roof gutters. I am quite comfortable.

My trunk has arrived and is waiting at the depot for me to pay the rest of the freight. I will be paid sometime and will get it then. In the meantime, I have enough.

I have cleaned the church and met with as many of the former members as I could. In the intervening years, some have joined the Methodist Church. There are a few families that have retained their membership but attended either the Roman or Lutheran Churches.

This morning, we sang Matins, with six in attendance. Their clear voices rang in the rafters. I am also going to write the bishop today and request that he come soon for a rededication service. I have not met any of the neighboring Episcopal priests; the nearest one is in Brookings. I hope to travel that way yet this summer.

The prairie is green and alive this time of year. I have enjoyed long walks in the country. There is a flatness that is constant, yet there is constant change.

Mother, you would love the sky here at dawn and dusk. The colors move in waves across the sky. The clouds are ablaze with color. And then suddenly it is all dark.

I told you of Ernst, Mr. Morland, who has befriended me. He and his daughter have cared for me since my arrival. I am eating with them. It is good, simple, farm food. The father has a depth that one rarely finds in men. His knowledge of scripture astounds me. You would enjoy their company. Underneath there is a sadness that quietly expresses itself. I have yet to find out what it is. Perhaps it is the loss of the mother.

Moreover, Mother, Miss Morland is the most beautiful woman I have ever seen. She is tall and willowy with red hair. Her pure heart is reflected in her blue eyes and creamy white complexion.

I have looked for a house for you and me. As of yet, I have not found one, but I believe that God will provide one for us. I hope to locate one with a bit of earth for us to till.

You may send your replies to me at General Delivery. I do not yet have an address.

Please rest each day with your feet up.

I remain,
Your loving son,
Jacob

* * * * *

May 18, 1947
Fr. Jacob Stewart
General Delivery
De Smet, South Dakota

Bishop Joseph Bradbury
Calvary Cathedral
Sioux Falls, South Dakota

Reverend Father,

I trust all is well with you.

I believe Bishop Taylor and the placement committee of the New York Diocese has written you that I would be serving at St. Stephen's parish in De Smet, South Dakota. I arrived at my parish on May 10 and have been occupied with cleaning and preparing it for use. I have met many of the former members, and hope to have the church, once again, full of worshippers.

One window was broken, and a sparrow made her nest in the reredos, tearing the tapestry. I do hope to find someone who can repair it.

This morning we sang Matins. I did not feel comfortable celebrating the Lord's Supper until you would be able to come and preside over the rededication of this building. When may I expect you?

I remain,
Your servant,
Jacob Stewart

* * * * *

May 18, 1947
Jacob Stewart
General Delivery
De Smet, South Dakota

Bishop P. Taylor
St. John the Divine
NYC, NY

Dear Bishop Taylor,

I am writing to inform you that I have arrived in South Dakota. I have followed your instructions and have been cleaning the church building and visiting the members and have found many of them receptive to the idea of reopening the church.

Today was our first service; we sang Matins, and I preached on Psalm 118:24. "This is the day the Lord hath made, I will rejoice and be glad in it." We can rejoice in the work that He has begun in De Smet.

I have written Bishop Bradbury; however, I have not heard from him. I trust he will come soon and bless the work here.

Please greet dear Mrs. Taylor for me.

Warmly,
Jacob

*P. S. Thank you once again for loaning me the money to travel. I
will reimburse you as soon as I am able. I will relate that the dreams
continue, and I am unable to sleep for more than a few hours at a
time. I had hoped the physical labor of cleaning the church would
wear my body out. I know that you pray for me. Please continue.*

* * * * *

Monday, May 19, 1947

Again, an unseasonably hot day, so the children were listless. I wish I were
a better teacher and knew what to do with them. They were not willing to do
anything but lay on their desks. After an unbearably hot morning, we went to
the basement and sat along the wall to read. The cement walls were cool and
damp. I heard a throat meaningfully cleared several times. Mr. Warren arrived
and cleared his throat again. "Miss. Morland, what are we doing in the basement? We have a classroom." We labored up to the heat.

I could not bear to face a hot supper, so I boiled eggs, and we had egg salad
sandwiches and some canned peaches.

At supper, the vicar said, "A very nice man stopped in today. I think his last
name was Wheezy?"

Dad just stared at his plate, so I blundered into it. "Was he tall, hooked
nosed, and starting to gray?"

"Yes, that was he. He offered to help with the repairs on the roof."

"That would be just like him."

After supper, while we were doing dishes, I decided to fill him in a bit
more. Even if Dad could not hear, I felt his disapproval. "Melvin Wiese grew
up on the farm next to ours. Now he owns much of the land surrounding our
farm, and he wants Dad to sell. Mr. Wiese seems very nice but is mean spirited
and covetous. His wife died a few years ago, and some say he is looking for a
new wife. We have chosen to have as little to do with him as possible. We are
not rude; we do not have a lot in common with Melvin or his family."

The vicar just looked at me and continued drying the dishes.

I do wonder if Dad heard it. He walked into the kitchen shortly afterward.

Tuesday, May 20, 1947

Dad brought in the wagon and filled the water barrels at the town well. I
watered my garden. The seedlings are wilted, and I think many have died in

this heat. What an odd spring! Only a week or so ago, we shivered in the cold and rain; today it was 90 degrees.

It seemed only appropriate that we would have wilted lettuce for supper.

Wednesday, May 21, 1947

Unbearably hot again. The fact that school will be out soon is my only relief from this heat. What will the summer be like?

Dad saw in the *Nordisk Tidende,* that tomorrow is the vicar's Name Day. So, we planned supper at the lake. I am not sure what we would do without the *Nordic Journal.* It keeps us up on the news in Norway and all things Norwegian. Every now and then Dad will see the name of one of his cousins and get excited. The best part is that during the war, it gave us factual news of what was happening in Norway.

Thursday, May 22, 1947
Name Day celebration for people named Jacob

At breakfast, I announced we were going to have supper at Lake Henry and roast hot dogs. I invited Mike and Marilyn, Jacob and Helen Hendricks, and their families to meet us at the lake. Marilyn brought potato salad, and Helen brought fresh buns. I made coleslaw and brought 48 hot dogs. I thought 48 would have been enough, but the big Hendricks boys went away hungry.

It took quite a bit of explaining before the vicar understood the importance of Norwegian Name Days. Once he realized what *navnedag* were about, he enjoyed the evening with Jacob. He liked the idea of a birthday and a Name Day. He thought the rest of America should catch on to it. He slipped and told us his birthday was October 22.

I was unsure what sort of gift to give for his Name Day, but I found some handkerchiefs on sale at Ward's Store. Both men seemed pleased with them.

After supper, the little children and ladies waded, while the men played catch with the boys.

It was hot again; I am glad it cools off at night.

Friday, May 23, 1947

Today was hot again.

It was also the last day of school. The children were too listless to enjoy any of the games.

Dad hauled water and watered my parched garden.

Mr. Warren came up to me and asked, "What are we doing this summer?" I know that he wants me to go to State Teacher's College in Aberdeen and get my four-year degree. I just do not know what to do. I would get more pay. But I would have to relinquish my job to any returning soldier that wanted it. Certainly, no returning soldier would want to teach first grade.

I took pity on the men and made a bigger supper. I am sure that lately I have sent them away hungry. In this heat, I have just not felt as if I wanted to eat or cook.

I opened a jar of meat, fried it, made gravy, and served it over rice. Along with the meat we had asparagus, lamb's quarters, dandelions, lettuce, and stewed rhubarb.

Saturday, May 24, 1947

Cleaning, gardening, resting. The heat was more bearable. Towards evening, there was a decided chill in the air.

After supper, Dad and I read on the porch. I wrapped up in a quilt.

When we were walking up the stairs to bed, we realized we had forgotten that tonight was the housewarming for Stanley and Louise. I have a couple of rugs from Peggy that I think they will like.

Sunday, May 25, 1947

Brisk with a stout north wind. Only a few days ago, it was unbearably hot.

We attended St. Stephen's again. I wonder if our own minister will call on us for being so negligent in our attendance. After all, we have missed two Sundays now.

The vicar's sermon was on the *Beatitudes;* it provoked some new thoughts.

Dad had invited the Gates and the Allens to join us for dinner. I was glad I picked up that nice pork roast yesterday at Pechel's.

I made pork roast, potatoes and gravy, canned beans, and applesauce cake for dinner.

Monday, May 26, 1947

Today dawned cold and it was misty all day. I stayed in all morning and worked on a new dress.

After lunch, I visited Mrs. Gehm. She was glad someone had braved the weather.

I decided not to light the furnace, since it could be hot tomorrow, but kept a fire going in the wood stove all day. I wore my tacky yellow chenille bathrobe over my dress. There was a tap at the back door; the vicar was there asking for a cup of tea. He made no comment, and I made no excuses for my attire. That gave me a comfortable feeling.

For supper, I opened the last jar of beef for beef and noodles. Now *that* made me feel weary, thinking about all the canning that lies ahead.

Wednesday, May 28, 1947

Last night, as we went to bed it began to rain. About 2 A.M., I woke to the wind howling. Dad had lit the furnace, but the house was an icebox. I got up, made tea, and sat in the kitchen with my feet propped on the oven door. It seemed as if my feet would never warm up.

Going back upstairs, I had just settled down to bed when there was noise in the kitchen. Dad must not have heard it, as he continued snoring. So gingerly I decided to investigate.

I pushed the door to the kitchen open and found the vicar making a cup of tea. He was shivering.

The howling wind and cold and now snow woke him in the basement of his church. He could not get warm. I am glad he knew that he would be welcome here.

I wrapped him in a quilt, pulled the rocker over close to the open oven, and sat him down. It was a bit before he was ready or able to talk.

I pulled another rocker up to the stove for myself. We sat side by side, rocking and listening to the wind. The vicar held his mug with both hands.

He talked of the winter of 1945 in Europe. Death. Wounded men lined up in rows in a church. Not enough supplies to treat them. He told me that he sees the dead in his sleep.

I must have dozed; I woke up with Dad making his presence known by coughing and standing between the rockers. "Good morning, Hanna. Good morning, Jacob." I quickly left to get dressed and then made oatmeal.

It was still gray outside, and the wind was still howling.

When the sun came out sufficiently to see, there were only two inches of snow. Ice covered everything. The trees hung low with the weight of the ice. I knew I would be indoors until it melted.

Dad and the vicar walked downtown and then out to the farm. They told me later they had both slipped several times.

They also reported many broken branches, cars in the ditches, downed REA lines and the train is not able to run. At Fuller's Hardware, they heard that the storm was worse further south. Everything was fine at the farm. The poor creatures were glad to see them.

I stayed inside and wore my tacky yellow chenille housecoat all day.

Dad thinks we need to move to the farm for the summer. With Uncle Edvard not there to watch over the animals, and my garden here has been ruined by this snowstorm, he said I could plant more out there.

Thursday, May 29, 1947

The vicar spent the night here at the house. Then today he and Dad put chains on the pickup and then went out to check on people further from town.

The sun came out, and the ice began to melt. You could hear it crack and pop as it fell off the trees and houses. Braving the weather, I went to check on Mrs. Gehm, then to Meyer's Butcher Shop for some meat. The lawns and bushes are green under the ice. There are broken limbs all over the place.

Mr. Meyer thinks the world is indeed coming to an end now. It was only two years ago that, with each development of the war, he also declared the end.

Friday, May 30, 1947
Memorial Day

Due to the storm, all the Memorial Day events are postponed until Sunday.

The vicar spent the night here again. At breakfast, he asked in whose room he had slept. Whose had it been? His question went unanswered. I am not certain if we ignored him or if we were waiting for the other to answer, or just did not want to talk about it.

The roads are muddy, and few can travel yet. I did hear the train arrive this morning. The paper is calling this the storm of the century.

Mr. Meyer called the college in Brookings to get the official temperatures for the month of May. It ranged from 90 at the first of the month to 25 degrees.

He has a chart made of butcher paper, now hanging in the window, with the temperatures and a Bible verse exhorting everyone to repentance.

I was reading it when Ina Roberts walked up and snorted that any good

Christian would never put up such a sign. He should have spent the money helping the poor instead of making long distance phone calls.

I asked her if we should each donate that same amount of money to the Kingsbury County Poor Farm. She coughed and said, "I give all my donations to my church where they do some good. People live at the poor farm because they are lazy. There is a reason the poor farm is on the far side of the county."

"Mrs. Roberts, what is that reason?"

"Young lady, you are far too much like your parents." Then she was gone. It is not clear what she meant by that, but I chose to take it as a compliment.

Saturday, May 31, 1947

I do not know if the end is near or not, but today seemed like a new beginning. The sun was warm, the ground is beginning to dry out, and much of my garden is looking surprisingly good. It seems that ice protected many plants. Of course, the tender ones are dead and need to be replanted. I do have more tomato and cucumber seeds.

Aunt Doris thinks the peonies will not bloom.

I cleaned the house in preparation for Sunday.

The vicar found some flags that had survived and brought a bouquet for the table and for the altar at St. Stephen's.

With the leftover roast, I made some soup.

Summer

Sunday, June 1, 1947

Today found us again at St. Stephen's. We sang Matins. I enjoy the comfortable similarity to our Lutheran services, but it is the sermons I like most. The vicar has a quiet way of exhorting us to greater depths in our faith.

Yesterday, Dad had killed a hen that he caught eating eggs, so I made chicken and dumplings with a few greens that had survived the storm.

Dad and I did not feel up to attending the Memorial Day service at the cemetery. Anyway, due to the storm there were no flowers to take.

Monday, June 2, 1947

Today as I was sweeping the front walk a great big girl came galumphing by. She had on lady's boots that were too large and missing the laces. She is large for her age, and her head always leans to her right, and her right arm dangles uselessly at her side. Her hair is dirty but combed; her dress was soiled and patched. I noticed the patching was done by someone who was not used to sewing. Her appearance hides a clear mind.

As she walked by, she turned her bright brown eyes to me and said, "Ma'am I seem to have lost my way. I was to get some bread and return right home."

After a bit of inquiry, I found she lived in the old Vincent house, behind the depot. I told her that I was going in that direction, and I would walk part way and point the way to her.

As we walked, she chattered away. Her name is Betty Jane and she will be in the fourth grade, and she loves to read, and her mother lets her read when her work is done and the triplets are behaving, and her mother is working at the De Smet Hotel as a maid, and her mother works hard and sleeps a lot, and had not worked for some time, and she did not know where her father was, and she liked poems, and her mother said she ate too much.

I told her I had lots of good books to loan to her and would be happy to do so and that she was welcome to stop by again.

Tuesday, June 3, 1947

I decided I needed something new to do so I walked downtown and bought transfer patterns and some fabric for fresh tea towels.

On the way as I passed St. Stephen's, the vicar was up on a ladder and my big galumphing girl from yesterday and three little sparrows were busy peppering him with questions.

He waved and looked pleadingly at me. I decided it was good for him to learn to talk to children, so I smiled and continued on my way.

I was in town longer than I planned; I ran into several people I had not seen for a while.

To my joy, on my way back, the galumphing girl and three sparrows were still annoying the vicar. However, this time he was sitting on the church steps with the girls lined up talking.

At supper, over fried chicken, and greens, I asked him about them. The three little girls are Galumphing Betty's sisters, the triplets, Lily and Rose and Violet. He said that the entire time they stood there at least one of them was talking.

He also said the three girls would be in my class this autumn. At this, his eyes crinkled, and he gave Dad a knowing look. I tried to act irritated at him but could not.

Wednesday, June 4, 1947

The vicar was quiet all during lunch. He asked Dad if he could walk with him to the farm.

Dad came home early and said that the vicar would be moving into the farmhouse. Could I get the house ready for him? Dad had to visit with the sheriff but would be home in time for supper. He did not have time to answer my questions but would later.

I made a quick bike ride to the farm to sweep out the worst of the dust, uncover the furniture, and make up the bed in the front room.

At supper, the two were very quiet. While we were washing dishes, the vicar told me he had received a letter that discouraged him. From the sounds of it, it would be discouraging to anyone. He is moving to the farm until this can be straightened out. Tomorrow he is going to look for work.

* * * * *

Bishop J. Bradbury
Calvary Cathedral
Sioux Falls, South Dakota

Fr. Jacob Stewart
General Delivery
De Smet, South Dakota

Dear Jacob Stewart,
I received your letter dated the 18th of May. I find this all very in-
teresting. I had not been notified that we were opening St. Stephen's.
I find this quite curious. I do not know where you got the key or
what your plans are.
I have also received a letter from an upstanding citizen of
De Smet who questions your integrity.
I must tell you that you are trespassing and that you need to lock
up the church and vacate the premises immediately. I will be con-
tacting the sheriff. Your failure to comply will result in your being
arrested.
Also, I prefer to be addressed as Your Grace. Please do so.
Sincerely,
His Holiness
Bishop Bradbury

* * * * *

Thursday, June 5, 1947
The vicar has found work. He will be working at the depot as the freight
handler. I think Dad must have put in a good word for him. Wages have gone
up since the war. He will be making a dollar an hour. Mr. Sweeney said he
should figure on at least fifty hours a week.

Dad brought home Jacob's trunk from the depot. He paid off the remaining
cost of the freight.

At supper, Dad told the vicar he had bought two tickets, and they could
leave Monday morning. The vicar was very insistent that it all be added to the
list of money he owes us for feeding him. Little does he know, but Dad probably hasn't started the list yet.

June 5, 1947
St. Stephen's Parish
General Delivery
De Smet, South Dakota

Bishop J. Bradbury
Calvary Cathedral
Sioux Falls, South Dakota

Your Grace,
I trust all is well with you.
I received your letter yesterday and wish to let you know that I have vacated the church of St. Stephen's. I have returned the key to where I found it.
I will be traveling to Sioux Falls as soon as possible to discuss this matter. I am sure it can be rectified.

I remain,
Your humble servant,
Fr. Jacob Stewart

* * * * *

Friday, June 6, 1947
The day of the "Mighty Endeavor." I have nothing but a heavy heart today.
I miss my brother. I miss Henry. I think of the Klucas family who lost two sons on this same day.

* * * * *

Fr. Jacob Stewart
General Delivery
De Smet, South Dakota
June 6, 1947

Bishop J. Bradbury
Calvary Cathedral
Sioux Falls, South Dakota

Your Grace,
I trust all is well with you.
I will be arriving in Sioux Falls on Monday, June 9, 1947, at
3 p.m. I trust you will have an opportunity to visit with me.
Most Sincerely,
Fr. Jacob Stewart

* * * * *

General Delivery
De Smet, South Dakota
June 7, 1947

Dear Mother,
I have a lot to relate and will do so in a letter soon. I have moved
into the Morland's farmhouse and will be working at the depot. The
farmhouse is a mile's walk north of De Smet.
I am fine. You can continue to send your letters to General
Delivery.

I am,
Your loving son,
Jacob

* * * * *

Sunday, June 8, 1947

The vicar walked into town, and we all walked together to St. Paul's
Lutheran Church.

I think he felt a bit funny as there were a few curious stares.

He was wearing his old suit. I asked him why he did not wear his new one
from his trunk. He said he was saving it.

"Dear" Mrs. Roberts came up to us and asked where we had been the past Sundays and who was our company? As Dad cordially introduced her to the vicar, Dad was his usual genial self.

Melvin Weise cornered Dad and talked about the changes in the congregation, Dad told me later that Melvin is one of the big pushers for the changes. I also heard Melvin Wiese say something about me, but I could not clearly hear what he said or Dad's reply.

If anyone can get under Dad's skin, it is Melvin Wiese. He thinks he is so much better, wiser, and more Christian than anyone. Sometimes I wonder if Dad ever says the wrong thing or feels different inside than what he portrays to others. What makes my dad so saintly?

Sunday dinner and then the afternoon was filled with plans for their trip. I baked bread and got a hamper of food ready.

Monday, June 9, 1947

The travelers left right after breakfast. I worked in the garden until the great Galumphing Betty and the three birdies came to visit. I did try to involve them in the weeding. Betty was helpful, but Lily and Rose and Violet were so busy talking and asking questions that I could not concentrate.

As they were leaving Betty shyly asked me if she could still borrow a book. We went in and selected *The Little House in the Big Woods,* one of Mrs. Wilder's books.

While in the kitchen Lily or Rose or Violet said that it must be getting close to dinner time and wondered what I was going to eat. Lily or Rose or Violet chimed in saying it would be nice to eat with me. We sat on the back porch, ate peanut butter sandwiches, and canned pears. Betty watched every move I made. The sparrows ate and talked without ever missing a beat. If one was not talking, it was only because her mouth was too full.

The girls were all wearing the same clothes they had on the other day. Betty still had on the pair of woman's shoes without laces. The goslings had on an assortment of ill-fitting shoes without laces, but their shoes appeared to fit better than Betty's.

I gave Betty a pair of laces, but she would not take them. "Mama don't 'low her to have no laces." Lily or Rose or Violet told me.

"Why can't she have laces?"

"Someone might eat them," was the reply of Lily or Rose or Violet. They looked at each other as if they couldn't believe that I was so dumb.

Sioux Falls Central Station
Sioux Falls, So. Dak.

Hanna,

We arrived here today at 3 P.M. We found a nice hotel within walking distance of the Cathedral. The Kensington—it is not as fancy as its name. There was a note on the door of the church office that they were closed for the day.

Dad

* * * * *

Tuesday, June 10, 1947
Old Settlers' Day!

Today was supposed to be the De Smet Ladies' Book Club meeting, but since it was Old Settlers' Day, our meeting was put off until next week. I had the house picked up and cookies ready in case anyone stopped in to see Dad. I do not think Dad has ever missed an Old Settlers' Day. It always surprises me how people come back every year for this.

I went to the parade and picnic lunch; it was lonely without Dad. A few of his old friends stopped in.

I met Marilyn and her family at the parade. She is planning a picnic for The Girls. She has decided we are making friendship quilts for each other. She has picked out the patterns and we will each make a block for all the other Girls.

Betty arrived, without the sparrows, in the late afternoon and asked for another book. I asked her questions about the one she had read, and I could tell she understood it.

I asked her about her shoes and dress. She quite frankly told me they were thankful to have what they did. It was hard for her mother to afford lots of clothes, and they grew too fast. She said that once they quit growing, they can then have more than one dress apiece.

I asked her to stand on some paper and traced her foot. She is to bring the sparrows tomorrow so I can trace their feet.

In the evening, I walked to the farm. Everything is in order. Hiram takes care of everything for us.

** * * * **

Sioux Falls Central Station
Sioux Falls, So. Dak.

Hanna,

I hope I can get this off today and you will get it in tomorrow's mail.

The bishop is in the western part of the state and will not be back until sometime towards the end of the week. We went to the church office. Jacob called it the Diocesan Office. There was an odd note on the door stating that it was closed, and that the bishop would not be back for a few days.

What was odd was an added sentence that said if anyone came from De Smet, they need not bother coming back.

Jacob knocked, but there was no answer. However, as we stood there discussing what to do next, we both saw the curtains move.

Much love,
Dad

** * * * **

Wednesday, June 11, 1947

I was barely finished with my tea when Galumphing Betty and the chickadees arrived. They chattered away and wanted to know why I was tracing their feet. I told them it was for school.

The girls then followed me around all morning and at noon hinted quite broadly that lunch on my porch would be delightful.

I took the foot tracings to Dakota Shoe Shop and tried to figure out what sizes they wore. Once Mr. Andus found out I was not going to buy the shoes from him, he was not too helpful. I really cannot blame him.

Then I went around the block to Mable's Secondhand Store and asked Mr. Mable when Mr. Anderson would be coming through next. He did not know.

I stopped at the De Smet Hotel hoping to meet the mother of Betty and Lily and Rose and Violet, but she was not there. The desk clerk could not find her. He did not know if she had come to work or not.

I took the pickup to the farm and worked in the garden, then gathered and sorted eggs. I dropped the eggs off at the egg station.

Later, while I was in the tub, I heard voices in the hall.

"I think she is home." "I wonder where she is." "Did she leave a snack for us?"

The chickadees were wandering around in the house looking for me. I hollered through the door at them to wait on the back porch.

* * * * *

Hanna Morland
305 Second Str.
De Smet, So. Dak.
June 11, 1947

Paul Anderson
492 Western Ave.
Sioux Falls, So. Dak.

Mr. Anderson,
　　I hope all is well with you and Peggy. Please give her my love.
　　When you come to De Smet, please bring a nice variety of serviceable fabrics (I will need at least 10 yards), and some sturdy shoes in the following sizes: 2 women's and 12 girls' (at least 3 pair).
　　Will you be bringing any books?
　　How is Peggy? I have quite a few balls of rug fabric ready for her.

I look forward to seeing you again.
Hanna Morland

* * * * *

Hanna Morland
305 Second Str.
De Smet, So. Dak.
June 11, 1947

Dear Peggy,
How are you? Dad and I are fine.
I am looking forward to spending the day with you when you are in De Smet.
I have many balls of rags for you, and I have saved all the Gasoline Alley comics since the last time I saw you, so bring your scrapbook, and we will paste them in.
Your friend,
Hanna

P. S. How do you like the silly picture of the dog on the front?

* * * * *

Thursday, June 12, 1947

I walked again to the De Smet Hotel to meet the mother of Galumphing Betty and Lily and Rose and Violet. She was actually there this time.

The conversation went something like this:

Me: Hello, I am Hanna Morland. I have met your girls and thought I would like to meet you.

Mrs. Speck: So?

Me: I think the triplets will be in my class this autumn.

Mrs. Speck: I pity you.

Me: They are all lively girls. They have been coming to see me almost every day.

Mrs. Speck: What do you want me to do about it?

Me: How do you like De Smet?

Mrs. Speck: It's a town.

Me: We attend St. Paul's Lutheran. You and your girls would be welcome any time.

Mrs. Speck: I work.

Me: Surely you get a day off.

Mrs. Speck: No.

Me: I wonder if you would mind if I helped with getting them some shoes and dresses.

Mrs. Speck: I don't care what you do.

Me: I was thinking of some used shoes and maybe a dress or two for school apiece.

Mrs. Speck: They will just wear them out. I get along fine without charity.

Me: But surely you would not mind if I got them a new dress and shoes.

Mrs. Speck: It's a free country; suit yourself. As I said, they will just ruin them. Do you have anything more you want to babble about? I have work to do.

Me: Well, it was nice to meet you. Welcome to De Smet. If you need anything or I can help, please let me know.

Mrs. Speck: Yeah.

As I walked away, I heard something about an uppity do-gooder.

Friday, June 13, 1947

Galumphing Betty and the ducklings were here again early this morning. I was working in the garden and heard their constant chatter. They stood at the front picket fence and talked to me. I tried to ignore them at first so that I could continue in the garden.

Finally, they left, only to walk around the block and come up the alley to talk.

"Ma'am I knew you couldn't hear us, so we's come around the back way," said Lily or Rose or Violet.

After "helping" me in the garden, they declared they were hungry and wondered if I had baked bread lately. So, we again had lunch on the back porch.

I did not want to spend my afternoon and evening worrying about Dad and the vicar, so I walked to the farm, cleaned that house, and worked in that garden. I sorted and boxed up Uncle Edvard's things. I will see if Mr. Anderson will take Uncle Edvard's clothes in trade. I carried it all up to what was formerly my bedroom. I saw that was where the vicar was staying, so then I went to put them in David's room. Grief kicked me in the pit of my stomach as I stepped in the door. Few of David's things were there, but the room was full of him and memories.

I stopped at Aunt Doris' house on the way home. After I had a good cry, she fed me what was left over from their supper.

I am tired. A hot bath, a good book, and my bed will be most welcome tonight.

Saturday, June 14, 1947

Yesterday, I also brought home the vicar's laundry, so I added that to ours. After the laundry was done, I set about to mend his clothing. I was mending his socks when I heard a gentle tapping on the door. It was Mr. Warren! I quickly smoothed my hair and answered. He was home for the weekend from Aberdeen and came to tell me about the wonderful classes he was taking and hoped I would join him the next session. Of course, it was said more like this: "We are having wonderful time learning and we wish that we would join us on our adventure."

I suggested we sit on the front porch, and I would serve him tea. And that also brought a most pleasant surprise. Mrs. B.! She was walking down the street with the back of her dress caught in the waistband of her bloomers. Her wide bottom and bloomers and garters were exposed to all. I wondered how I could discreetly tell her what she was revealing to the entire world?

Seeing us on the porch, she turned in at the gate and came up to the porch.

"Isn't this lovely? Two little lovebirds sipping tea."

Oh, that caused such a struggle. Which would embarrass Mrs. B. more? To tell her, or not tell her? If I told her in front of Mr. Warren, she would be embarrassed. If I waited and did not tell her, then she could be further humiliated by walking the rest of the way home displaying her bloomers.

Well, Galumphing Betty and Lily and Rose and Violet solved the problem. They came walking by and shouted at her, "Hey Lady, your dress is stuck up in your shorts and yer showing your butt to the world."

She quickly pulled her dress out and fled.

I was on the front porch after supper, still mending the vicar's clothes and hoping to catch a glimpse of Dad walking from the depot. Instead, Mrs. B. came to see me.

"I knew all along that my dress was hiked up. That Mr. Warren is such a fuddy duddy; I wanted to give him the shock of his life."

Here I decided to be kind. "I am sure he was shocked," was all I said.

Then she starts examining my mending. "Oh, getting a little comfortable with two men. I see."

I gave her a blank look, hoping she would move on to a new topic. Nope. She could not be detoured.

"Receiving one and serving him tea on the porch when your father is gone. And then you are doing mending for the other."

After she left, I daydreamed about the possibility of being Mrs. William Jennings Bryan Warren. We started to wonder if we would be sane for very long.

Sunday, June 15, 1947
Father's Day and Dad's Birthday

I will have to celebrate the day when he gets home.

The radio and Sioux Falls newspaper have been full of the anniversary of the liberation of the concentration camps, reviewing the details and interviewing the survivors. I can hear and read no more. It weighs too heavy.

It was a long, lonely Sunday. I walked to Aunt Doris' after church. She fed me lunch, and then I walked all the way to Marilyn's farm. Nothing felt comfortable. I then walked quite far on the Manchester road, hoping to wear out my mind and body.

Monday, June 16, 1947

I tossed and turned all night, waking up sore and cranky.

Dad and the vicar arrived on the afternoon train. I was so glad to see Dad coming down the walk that I fairly flew off the steps to greet him, just as I did when I was a girl, and he came home from the farm.

Over tea, Dad told me of their adventures. The bishop was not available at first, so they went to Canton to see Aunt Julia and her family. He had so many greetings and hugs, for me, from them all. The bishop was supposed to be back when they returned to Sioux Falls, but there was another note that said he had continued west to visit some of the Indian churches. They waited a day, and he did not return. They decided to come home. Dad said the vicar was especially discouraged.

The vicar arrived in time for supper. Afterward, he insisted that Dad go over the account of the money that he owes us for food, his trunk, and the other things for which we have paid.

Dad was willing to be kind and forget much of the debt, but the vicar was quite exacting on what he owed and when he would pay it. Dad wanted to let him live at the farm for free, telling him he was doing us a favor by living there and keeping watch over the place.

Over tea and strawberry-rhubarb pie we talked a little of Europe and the war. The vicar stared off in space and was lost in thought. Dad wisely changed the subject.

The vicar will return to his job at the depot tomorrow.

* * * * *

Fr. Jacob Stewart
General Delivery
De Smet, South Dakota
June 17, 1947

Bishop P. Taylor
St. John the Divine
New York City, New York

My dearest friend,

I experienced the most frustrating week. It was so difficult not to become upset.

I really do not know where to begin. Since arriving here in De Smet, I have been busy with cleaning the parish building, visiting members, and having services. I wrote Bishop Bradbury several times introducing myself, asking his advice, and requesting that he come and bless the work that has begun here.

Then, I received a letter from him, telling me he had never heard of you or from you and that I should vacate the church, or he would notify the authorities. Mr. Morland checked this out with the sheriff, and the sheriff had not yet received a call.

I thought this was a simple mistake that would be straightened out with a personal visit. This last week, I traveled to Sioux Falls only to find the bishop on an extended journey to inspect the Indian Missions.

I will write to him tonight and if, dear sir, you could also write to him and help solve this mystery that would be helpful and much appreciated.

Please explain to him that I am not mistaken, but that I did receive a commission to pastor St. Stephen's.

Presently I am fulfilling my calling by unloading freight at the depot.

Jacob Stewart

P. S. You requested that I tell you when I have struggles. On the anniversary of D Day, the newspaper published a picture of rows upon rows upon rows of dead men lying on the beach. My nightmares have increased, and I am especially weary from the lack of sleep.

*****

Jacob Stewart
General Delivery
De Smet, South Dakota
June 17, 1947

Dearest Mother,

How are you? Are you keeping your feet up?

You will need to pray for me and the situation here. I am a bit discouraged. However, I am glad that I am not in charge and can leave it up to the Lord.

It seems that Father Taylor's letter to the local bishop got lost and now the local bishop questions my integrity. I am sure it will be straightened out soon. Please continue to pray.

I have found employment at the depot as a freight handler. It is not easy work, as there is a lot of freight that arrives here and then is taken to nearby towns. Mr. Sweeney, the station master, seems to like me as I have followed father's and your advice to do more than is expected. I start my day by making him a pot of coffee and then sweeping the station. We are getting along fine.

I am living at the Morland's farm. It has a small four room cottage without running water or electricity. Mr. Morland says the REA lines will be coming through that area sometime in the future.

The main floor has only a kitchen and bedroom, divided by a stairway, leading to two small bedrooms upstairs. The bedroom on

*the main floor was made up for me, but I decided to sleep upstairs. I
selected the bedroom on the east, a cheery room with yellow flow-
ered wallpaper. It must have been Miss Morland's. I will be quite
comfortable there. By the window are an old rocker and a table, so I
can sit and watch the sunrise as I have my morning devotions.*

*The farmyard has several outbuildings, a large barn, a chicken
house, and a summer kitchen.*

*Their house in town is more substantial than this cottage and is
also comfortable. I particularly like the kitchen and back porch. The
kitchen is a large sunny room where Mr. Morland and his daughter,
Ernst and Hanna. do most of their living. It is as modern as any
kitchen you would find in New York except that in the corner is an
old wood burning range. They use that to heat and cook when the
electricity goes out.*

*I will probably be attending church with the Morlands. They are
Lutherans (here Mr. Morland would remind me that they are
Norwegian Lutherans, to him that is crucial). He has explained to
me, several times, that the Norwegian Lutheran Church has always
been a confessional church and that now the church is moving toward experiential. (I do not fully understand this.)*

Keep me in your prayers. I am doing well.

I just wish you were here to add to my joy.

I remain,

Your loving son,

Jacob

✳ ✳ ✳ ✳ ✳

Tuesday, June 17, 1947

This will be the last day the vicar will be here for breakfast. He said he can
fry an egg and make toast. I am not sure he is used to cooking on a wood burning stove, so I suggested he do his cooking in the summer kitchen on the
kerosene stove. He will learn.

The vicar has only half an hour for lunch, so I sent one in an old lard pail.
He said that once he gets paid, he may eat lunch at one of the cafés. Until then,
either Dad or I will drop off a dinner pail at the depot.

I was out hoeing in the garden and could hear a faint, "Woo-whoo are we
busy?"

Ahh, we were again visited by Mr. Warren. I am not sure why he is back so soon.

I was polite. I do want to get along with him. I must work with him. I need to let him know in some way, without hurting his feelings, that I am not interested in dating him or marrying him.

I wonder if Dad will talk to him for me.

I did stop hoeing and visit. Mr. Warren hinted that he would like a cup of tea, but I ignored it.

The De Smet Ladies' Book Club met this afternoon. We continued to discuss the *Pavilion of Women* that we started last month. Next month we will read *Betsy in Spite of Herself* by Maud Hart Lovelace. Maud is such a gentle writer; I think we will all enjoy it.

Mrs. Andus served lemon cake, a *Your Neighbor Lady* recipe. Mrs. B. announced that Wynn Speece will be at the State Fair in Huron; she was going to see her if she has to walk there.

And as usual, Mrs. B. knew about the visit from Mr. Warren. Before she left, she made several comments about what a nice catch he was. All the while she said this, she wriggled her eyebrows at me. Mrs. Williams stifled a laugh. Later Mrs. Williams called and told me that when Mrs. B. was wiggling her eyebrows, it looked like two black caterpillars crawling across her forehead.

Wednesday, June 18, 1947

I walked to the post office; Mrs. Roberts and Mrs. B. were there. Sometimes I even surprise myself, I was cordial. I wished them, "God dag."

They sidled up to me and offered advice for getting rid of lice. Since I was with those little urchins so much, I would surely get lice. I thanked them and said I had not had lice since fourth grade when the whole class caught them from you, Mrs. B.

However, all the way home my scalp itched. I tried not to scratch. Once back home, I quickly washed my hair in some good strong soap.

Thursday, June 19, 1947

Marilyn picked me up before noon, and we met The Girls at Spirit Lake for a picnic. We waded, splashed, and swam.

We were each to bring something to eat that began with the same letter as our first name. There was quite an assortment. Besides my ham ball, there were Marilyn's meatballs, Blanche's baked beans, Carol's carrots, Emma's eggnog, Susan's cottage cheese salad, Alice's applesauce, and Irma's Irish Soda Bread. We laughed over the menu until our sides ached.

Marilyn handed out quilt patterns. She wants each of us to make eight blocks, with our names embroidered on them, and we will exchange them. She has set January 15 as the date we are to be done.

When the vicar came for supper, he had an old, rusted lunch pail, of which he seemed quite proud. When Mr. Wilke gave it to him, he told him that since he was a real railroader now, he needed a real railroader's lunch pail. It is quite unique; it has a cup on the top and several different trays that fit inside. He plans on cleaning it up and using it.

Today, *Your Neighbor Lady,* Wynn shared a Chow Mein recipe. I tried it and it turned out to be tasty. Dad said I could make it again. Today was the ninth anniversary of Your Neighbor Lady appearing on the radio. She has been our constant friend all these years. I wonder what we did without her.

Friday, June 20, 1947

Melvin Wiese came to visit Dad, and they stood by the pickup for some time. I do not know why or what they talked about. I know, in the past, Melvin Wiese tried to buy our farm. He is a greedy man.

Dad was agitated when he came in. At supper, he snapped at the vicar and me when we were arguing.

Saturday, June 21, 1947
Sommersolverv

I feel quite good about myself today. I got the house cleaned and did several loads of laundry. It was such a pleasant, sunny day the clothes dried quickly.

The vicar was paid today and asked if he could splurge by taking us to supper. We went to the Ever Open Cafe.

Afterward the vicar and Dad sat on the back porch and drank coffee. I went upstairs and was cleaning in the back bedroom. I had not meant to eavesdrop, but their whole conversation floated up to me.

Dad told him of Melvin Wiese telling people quite adamantly that our St. Paul's Church needs to merge with the two south country churches and make one new church. Dad said Melvin is making unbelievably strong statements, such as saying all true Christians will back his plan.

Five carloads of local young married couples traveled from here to Dalesburg for the Summer Solstice Celebration and a baseball tournament. It would have been fun to go along, but I would have been the only old maid.

We sat on the front porch and watched the sun go down; it did not get dark until 10 P.M.

Sunday, June 22, 1947

It has been a week, and still the vicar has not heard anything from his bishop.

The vicar came by and went with us to church. It is funny, there is no more rationing of gas, but we still walk just about everywhere. We are two blocks from downtown, five from church, six from school, and one mile from the farm.

After dinner, Melvin Wiese stopped in. I told him Dad was napping, and I would wake him, but he said he would be just as happy to visit with me. We sat on the porch, and I listened politely, oohing and ahhing when appropriate. I tried to smile. He mostly talked about his money, himself, and his children.

I was so glad when Galumphing Betty and the goslings came and took over the conversation. Shortly after their arrival, Melvin Wiese hacked and coughed and said he had to leave.

Wednesday, June 25, 1947

Dad was cutting hay all day and came in quite tired. I offered to drive the tractor tomorrow, but he said he would be rested up after a good night's sleep.

The poor vicar! He was quiet. He told us about a letter he had received today from the bishop. He says he is not worried because he knows the truth and that will stand for itself. He *is* concerned about these local people that have registered their complaints with the bishop and what he had done to cause it.

After supper and dishes, he left for the farm.

* * * * *

Bishop Bradbury
Calvary Cathedral
Sioux Falls, South Dakota
June 25, 1947

Jacob Stewart
General Delivery
De Smet, South Dakota

Jacob Stewart,
I will be making a tour of the missions in the Sisseton area shortly. I will be in De Smet to assess the damage that you have caused to our dear St. Stephen's Church. Please be prepared to visit with the sheriff and make monetary reimbursement for the damage you have heaped upon Church property.
I will also be meeting with the local people that have registered complaints about your behavior.
Sincerely,
His Holiness
Joseph Bradbury
Bishop
Sioux Falls Diocese

* * * * *

Friday, June 27, 1947
David's Birthday

David would have been 29 today. Neither Dad nor I said anything about it until I served David's favorite coconut custard pie with our coffee. Dad sat and looked at it with watery eyes. Then, with achy throats, we reminisced about days gone by. At my age, I do not often get hugs from my dad, but tonight I got a good night hug.

Saturday, June 28, 1947

There were only two early freight trains expected today, so the vicar got permission to help at the farm after they were unloaded. He and Dad baled hay all day. With the vicar working on the trailer and stacking the bales, the work went much quicker.

I spent the day at the farm, cooking, cleaning the house, and working in the chicken house. We came home in the pickup. I do not think I could have walked back home after today.

Sunday, June 29, 1947

Pastor announced that on Wednesday there would be a meeting for all voting members of the congregation. At that point, Melvin Wiese turned and looked at us, with a steely eyed look and stare. Dad sat looking straight ahead, ignoring him.

Monday, June 30, 1947

Well, the long awaited day arrived. Bishop Bradbury came to St. Stephen's and visited with the vicar. I understand he was quite thorough in his investigation. He interviewed Dad, Mr. Sweeney the depot agent, several businessmen, members of the congregation, and Melvin Wiese.

He concluded that the vicar did not do any damage to the building, but he was not ready to give assent to having services there until he hears from the placement committee in New York. The vicar said he showed him the letter from the Bishop of New York, but that was not good enough. The bishop was confident it was forged. He spent the night in the De Smet Hotel.

Dad so seldom says anything bad about anyone but mentioned at supper that he was very uncomfortable during the interview. He felt the bishop was hiding something.

Tuesday, July 1, 1947

Dad and I picked up bales. I drove the tractor, and he loaded them. After work, the vicar loaded bales, Dad drove, and I made supper. I picked raspberries and served them with cream.

They got all the hay in by sunset. That feels good.

Driving home, I could not believe my eyes. We saw Mrs. Speck out for a stroll with a short, dignified gentleman who was wearing a derby; Dad said it was the bishop. I wonder what in the world they would have in common.

Wednesday, July 2, 1947

Galumphing Betty and Lily and Rose and Violet came by today. They told me their mother had spent the night at the hotel, cheering up a sad preacher. My jammers! What is that supposed to mean?

The vicar went home right after supper.

Dad went to the church meeting. I knew I would not be able to concentrate on anything, so I told Dad to pick me up at Aunt Doris's after the meeting. I took my redwork along to do. When I tried to embroider, it was all knots, so I put it away.

We tried to talk about several different topics but continued to return to the members' meeting. She feels that if women had the right to vote, we would make the right decisions. She wonders if women will ever get the right to vote in church matters.

We fell asleep waiting for the men. Dad and Uncle Bob came in after 11 P.M. At first, they did not want to tell us anything, but Aunt Doris bribed them with Red Velvet Cake.

I guess it was a heated discussion. Since we have been supplying a pastor to the two country churches, the men voted that those churches needed to pay more toward the pastor's salary or find their own pastors. It is a way to pressure them into combining with us. The plan calls for three old church buildings to be torn down and one new one to be built on land owned by Melvin Wiese. He has some slough ground on the southwest corner of town that he offered the congregation at a "good price."

The combined churches will then join with the American Synod.

We did not need to ask how they voted. It was obvious, Uncle Bob and Dad voted against the whole thing. The two country churches will not have a choice; with so many people leaving the farms and moving to town, they have had a hard pull of it. All three buildings that we have worshiped in for three generations will become firewood.

Dad is most adamant that we should not join the American Synod but remain in the Norwegian Synod.

Uncle Bob kept imitating Melvin Wiese saying. "this is the wave of the future and those that are against it are against progress and Christianity." Melvin Wiese also repeated that all families from the "true homesteaders" will be for the change.

Three generations later, he is still pointing out who homesteaded and who bought a relinquishment.

Thursday, July 3, 1947

I decided to figure this church issue out for myself. I borrowed several church doctrine books from the church library and have them set up on the kitchen desk. I will read in the doctrine books and check out every verse in the Bible to see if that is what the Bible is saying and take notes. I need to understand what is a confessional church.

At supper, the vicar asked us if we had heard any good gossip today. We both looked at him in surprise. He was smiling. He then went on to tell us that Melvin Wiese had been in the depot and informed the station master that the state is going to pave the Huron road and make it a highway. He says it already has a number, and runs by some land he owns. It will be called Highway 14. It is interesting that it runs past where Melvin Wiese wants to build the new church and by another piece of property he owns.

Friday, July 4, 1947
Independence Day!

A day of rest, a parade, and a picnic! I made fried chicken, potato salad and a chocolate cake to take. It was so good to see all the old friends and family again. There were seven freezers of ice cream, and still not enough to go around.

In the afternoon there were the usual ball games. I was surprised when the vicar joined in. He hit a home run; he plays quite well. Maybe he has more talents than we know.

After dark, we sat with Betty and Lily and Rose and Violet and watched the fireworks.

After walking the girls home, the vicar asked if he should escort me home. I told him I could take care of myself.

Saturday, July 5, 1947

I cleaned the house and got ready for Sunday company.

Dad took the dinner pail to the depot, so I did not see the vicar until supper. I felt so unnerved that I could not look at him. I am just not sure how I feel about him asking to escort me home.

Supper was a little meager, with deviled eggs, the first ripe cucumbers, boiled beets, and bread and butter.

Dad and I listened to the *Missouri Valley Barn Dance* until bedtime. It is so funny; we used to listen to the radio every night to hear news of the war. Now, several days will go by before we turn it on.

As we were walking upstairs, he asked if I wanted to go to one of the country churches tomorrow instead of our church. He even suggested the Methodist church. I was a bit surprised but said I would go wherever he wanted.

Sunday, July 6, 1947

The vicar had said he would meet us at church, and we had no way of telling him we would be going to a different church, so Dad decided to go to St. Paul's instead.

Dad called and invited the Gates and the Allens over for dinner. I had a pot roast, mashed potatoes, gravy, macaroni salad, green beans, and raspberry pie.

They did question us about the upcoming church merger and new building. And the Gates had heard about the new highway being planned.

They both also told the vicar that when they had met with his bishop, they only said positive things and hoped the church would be open again soon.

Monday, July 7, 1947

After breakfast, Dad called the telephone company and asked that the phone be hooked up at the farm again.

On the way to the farm, we dropped the dinner pail off at the depot and noticed David's bicycle leaning against the wall. At supper, the vicar apologized; he said he didn't think we would mind. Dad said he was glad someone was using it. It is surprising that the tires are still good.

The vicar saw my Bible and the doctrine books out on the desk in the kitchen and wondered what I was doing. After I explained he said, "Good for you."

In the morning, I picked raspberries and then washed and canned them in the summer kitchen. As usual, the kerosene stove was a bit temperamental, but I got the berries all done by midafternoon. I saved two gallons of berries for jam.

At about 5:00, Galumphing Betty and Lily and Rose and Violet came by. They kept asking me about Terry and the Pirates. It took me quite a bit to understand that they wanted to listen to Terry and the Pirates on the radio. So, we settled into the kitchen with a glass of milk each. I have never seen them so quiet.

Tuesday, July 8, 1947

After such a wild spring, the weather has settled down to a comfortable, regular pattern. We have received rain each time we needed it. I made and canned raspberry jam this morning.

The afternoon was taken up by The De Smet Ladies' Book Club. Most of the ladies liked *Betsy in Spite of Herself.*

Mrs. Williams served angel food cake and raspberries. It was plain, simple, and tasty. She got an electric mixer for her birthday and enjoyed using it to beat the egg whites. Of course, as soon as Mrs. Walters and her band of biddies left, we all went into the kitchen for a demonstration.

At 5 P.M. Galumphing Betty and Lily and Rose and Violet arrived to listen to Terry and the Pirates. They said their mother had to work late, so I invited them for supper. I had planned there would be leftovers for lunch tomorrow, but that did not happen. They fairly devoured the salmon loaf and peas.

Dad says the wheat is turning and we will be harvesting soon.

* * * * *

Bishop Bradbury
Calvary Cathedral
Sioux Falls, South Dakota

J. Stewart
General Delivery
De Smet, South Dakota

Jacob Stewart,

If that is really your name.

I will be returning to De Smet on Wednesday, July 16. Please book a room at the De Smet Hotel for me. I will be far too busy visiting with the fine citizens of De Smet to interview you. As of yet, I have not received any information from New York about you and your so called placement in De Smet.

Please refrain from sending a message to me at the Diocesan Office. I will just trust that you have made the reservations.

Sincerely,
His Holiness
Joseph Bradbury
Bishop
Sioux Falls Diocese

Wednesday, July 9, 1947

I picked gooseberries and made a *stikkelsbær krydderkake.* Then I went to the farm and cleaned and sorted eggs. There were enough to bring them into the egg station. We continue to sell ours to the Cream City Creamery, even when the train depot is offering more per dozen.

It was a bit warm today so this afternoon I took my handwork and sat out under the tree. Galumphing Betty, and Lily and Rose and Violet joined me. I asked them a bit more about their mother, but I could only get out of them that she cleans at the hotel and sometimes helps people sleep. If a hotel guest is having trouble sleeping, she will give them a back rub.

They wanted to listen to *Terry and the Pirates* again. I shooed them off before supper. Dad wondered if they ate regularly and if I should not plan to feed them at least one meal a day.

The vicar told us he had received a letter and that the bishop was returning next week. He said he found the message perplexing but didn't elaborate.

Thursday, July 10, 1947

I decided I would again try and talk to Mrs. Speck, the mother of Galumphing Betty and Lily and Rose and Violet. She was not at the hotel and could not be found, so I went to her house, but she was not there either. The girls said she was at work. For some reason, they would not open the door and only talked to me through the broken screen.

Meanwhile back at the hotel, Mr. Spurgeon told me Mrs. Speck comes and goes and as long as she continues to do such a good job cleaning, he does not care. She is paid by the room anyway.

Mrs. B. was at the post office and told me that Princess Elizabeth had announced her engagement. I had to stifle a giggle. She related this to me in a way as if she were telling me news about someone we both knew. I wondered if she was expecting an invitation to the royal wedding.

Friday, July 11, 1947

Green beans filled my day, my hands, my jars, and will probably fill my dreams. I canned 48 quarts today. I do not want to see another bean, so I pulled out all but one row. I will save that much.

But that is far from the highlight. Hot, sweaty, and tired, I made supper. Green beans and ham! I also had some bread and apple sauce. But shortly before we sat down to supper, we came tapping at our door!

Mr. William Jennings Bryan Warren came to tell us about his time in Aberdeen. I was hoping that Dad would send him on his way. No! We were invited to supper.

I hoped that he would not be so pompous around Dad and the vicar, but he was.

However, after supper, he did have an almost normal conversation with Dad about education and what he was learning at Northern.

As he was leaving, he made a plea with Dad about my attending the last session of summer classes.

Dad wondered later if I would enjoy that, three weeks away, time to read, rest, and study. It sounds quite tempting, but there is so much to be done here in the next month that I do not know how I could ever leave him with all that work.

Saturday, July 12, 1947

Again, at breakfast, Dad brought up my going to Aberdeen. I got a piece of paper and started a list of everything I needed to do in August.

After supper, Dad and I went to the ball field to watch the game. The De Smet Pioneers are playing Lake Preston. I was surprised to see the vicar playing first base. Dad said that after playing with them on the Fourth they had asked him to join the team.

Sunday, July 13, 1947
Aunt Julia's birthday!

Dad and I had entirely forgotten. I could not believe it when he called her long distance! She is doing well and sounded in good spirits.

He wondered if I wanted to take a vacation instead and go spend a couple of weeks in Canton with Aunt Julia and her family; or if I would like to go to Augustana College in Sioux Falls and take classes.

I asked him if he was trying to get rid of me.

"No, I need you like a dog needs fleas," was his response.

Mr. Warren was in church this morning, which is unusual, since he is a

Methodist. When we walked in, he was loitering in the entryway and followed us in and sat next to me. I was surprised at what a fine singing voice he has. Mr. Warren stayed for Bible class but did not make any comments.

Afterward, Mrs. B. came up and wriggled her eyebrows at me and made kissing noises. I was not kind. I stared at her as hard and mean as I could. She just laughed and walked away. Later, I saw her talking to Dad and giggling worse than a schoolgirl.

Monday, July 14, 1947

Why was I totally astonished when Mrs. B. came to see me today? She wondered if I had a cup of vanilla she could borrow. I told her I could spare a few tablespoons, but she left without it.

In the meantime, she did tell me she was glad I was dating Mr. Warren instead of that hairy preacher. Mr. Warren was so handsome, dignified, and witty. She wondered if I had time to plan a wedding before school started and offered any help she could give.

It is time to start harvesting winter wheat. Dad has been quiet. It will be the first harvest without Uncle Edvard. When I asked Dad about Uncle Edvard, his eyes teared up. So, I changed the subject.

He has hired Ben Peterson to help, who is a good worker, but can he eat. It will be like cooking for a whole crew.

Tuesday, July 15, 1947

As I walked to the farm, I walked past the depot; Mrs. B. was talking to the vicar. I waved, but they did not notice me.

I drove the horses and the rake. When I looked back and saw how straight my rows were, I was a bit proud.

Dad said it was time we bought a second tractor. We are some of the last to even keep horses.

I fixed supper in the summer kitchen. The vicar said he would be glad to eat with us when I came to the farm to make supper for Dad, but he would be doing all his own cooking from now on. He was making enough money at the depot and could buy his own groceries, and he did not want to be a bother. There was a hint of sadness in his voice and eyes when he said it. My first thought was Mrs. B., what did she say to him this morning?

I opened my mouth to protest, but Dad spoke up with, "Well, Jacob, it is your decision."

I made fried chicken and gravy, mashed potatoes, green beans, tomatoes, and cucumbers. Then the vicar amended his comments, he would be glad to eat a meal like that any time.

The combining is going well. But, as usual, Dad had to stop and do some repairs. I think he would like one of those new self-propelled combines.

Wednesday, July 16, 1947

Galumphing Betty and Lily and Rose and Violet were here most of the day. They walked to the farm and helped gather, sort, and clean eggs. Betty is a hard worker and did well. I gave them a dozen eggs for their help, but they refused them and said I could "fry 'em up" for them tomorrow.

They said their mother would be busy all day helping a preacher.

Dad threshed all day with Ben, then the vicar rode the thresher after supper. The straw was getting too tough, so he quit at about 9. It is humid; I hope it does not rain.

The bishop was supposed to be visiting here today, but the vicar could not find him, and the desk clerk would not answer him as to whether the bishop was here or not.

Thursday, July 17, 1947

Again, the girls were here. Their mother was helping a preacher again. I fried up half a dozen eggs for lunch. They must not have eaten any breakfast and were so hungry, so I cooked the rest.

I tried to question them about their mother and their past, but if Lily or Rose or Violet started to answer Betty would give them a warning look.

No rain, hot and humid all day. It feels as if the sky could open and downpour any second.

Dad was pleased with the progress of his threshing. I walked out and drove a load of wheat to the elevator. Afterward, I made supper in the summer kitchen again; the vicar joined us and then drove the thresher.

* * * * *

Fr. Jacob Stewart
General Delivery
De Smet, South Dakota
July 17, 1947

Bishop Bradbury
Calvary Cathedral
Sioux Falls, South Dakota

Your Grace,

I was hoping that I would have been able to visit with you when you were here on July 16. I stopped by the De Smet Hotel and inquired. However, they would not tell me if you had been able to come to De Smet.

I hope your investigation was completed and that you will be able to give your blessing to my ministry here.

I look forward to visiting with you again soon. Should I come to Sioux Falls so that we can continue our discussion? Have you received word from the placement committee?

I remain,
Your servant,
Jacob Stewart

* * * * *

Friday, July 18, 1947

The winter wheat harvest is all done, and soon Dad will start on the oats.

Promptly at 5:00 the girls came and sat on the back porch. This has become our afternoon ritual. They sit on the porch until I invite them in for a glass of milk and cookies or bread and jam. They chatter and giggle and wriggle and smack their lips until 5:15. When I turn on the radio, it is so quiet you could hear a pin drop as we listen to the adventures of *Terry and the Pirates*.

I made a basket supper and took it out to the farm on my bike, beef stew, coleslaw, tomatoes, cucumbers, and a raspberry pie. I made the stew in my largest Jewel Tea casserole dish, and it made the trip just fine. I heated it up in the summer kitchen.

Dad handed the stew to Ben first, who helped himself to almost half of it. The three of us then shared the other half, which means Ben ate 3/6, and we each ate 1/6. I was glad for the vegetables to fill up on.

Saturday, July 19, 1947

Oat harvest is going well. Dad stopped at 4. Ben and the vicar had a ball game to go to. The De Smet Pioneers played the Willow Lake Pirates at Willow Lake this evening. Dad wondered if we should drive up and watch. But after supper, he sat in his rocker and fell asleep.

The news is full of those poor Jews on the Exodus. I do not understand why the British just do not let them go to Palestine. Have the Jewish people not suffered enough?

Sunday, July 20, 1947

Oh my! After lunch, Dad sat down with a pen and the list that I had made of all the things that I had to do in the next month and told me how he had taken care of the list.

What about all the canning?
> ▸ Aunt Julia would do the canning. She would be coming to spend the month here and take care of everything.

How do you know she would come and do the canning?
> ▸ I called and asked her.

What? You made two long distance calls in one month?
> ▸ Yes.

Who would take care of the gardens?
> ▸ Jacob and I will take care of them.

Who will sew clothes for Betty and Lily and Rose and Violet?
> ▸ I asked Marilyn, Aunt Doris, and Mrs. Gehm to organize this, and they were glad to help sew.

You asked Mrs. Gehm to help?!
> ▸ Yes, Mrs. Gehm. She was glad to have something to do. She thought she could do all the handwork on the hems.

Who would do the cleaning and laundry?
> ▸ I do not make much of a mess. I also hired Mrs. Callahan to come help.

She won't take money.
> ▸ I think she will take it from me.

The vicar, who will take care of him?

> ▸ He is a grown man and can take care of himself.

You…who is going to manage you?

> ▸ I can manage myself quite nicely, thank you.

Dresses…I have nothing to wear!

> ▸ Aunt Doris and Marilyn have both agreed to help you sew.

Who was going to do Aunt Julia's canning?

> ▸ Her daughters are home and will take care of everything while she comes and helps here.

How will we ever pay for these classes?

> ▸ We have plenty of money for this. Remember we had a bumper wheat crop.

I will miss you.

> ▸ Yes, and I will miss you.

I ran out of arguments. He probably had more answers.

He had called Aberdeen (*three* long distance phone calls!); the classes that are taught during those three weeks are Diagnosing Reading Difficulties and The Primary Classroom. The person he talked to told him of a boarding house nearby where I would be comfortable and safe.

He called and talked to the lady who runs it and feels it would be an excellent place to stay. (He made *four* long distance phone calls!)

The conversation ended with him telling me that it is entirely up to me.

I am excited and scared to take college classes, worried that I won't be missed, concerned about being off by myself and the work not getting done and leaving a workload for others.

Monday, July 21, 1947
Name Day for Johannes

I woke up and realized I was going to Aberdeen. *I am going to college!*

I thought often of my dear Bestemor today, on her name day. I think she would be as excited as I am about my going to college.

At breakfast, Dad said I was to go to Ward's Store and pick out enough fabric for four new dresses. I called Aunt Doris and Marilyn, and they met me there to help pick it out.

Uncle Bob was supposed to bring Aunt Doris' machine over here. He decided that he was not going to haul her treadle "all over God's creation," so he bought her an electric sewing machine! She was so surprised when she walked in and saw it in the kitchen with a red bow on it.

We started sewing right after lunch.

Dad continued thrashing oats today. The vicar helped after work.

Tuesday, July 22, 1947

Aunt Doris and Marilyn were here again all day to help sew. The kitchen was whirring with the clacking of my treadle machine. The electric machines purred so quietly. With all three of us sewing, we got two dresses done.

For lunch, we each contributed something. Aunt Doris brought some fried chicken; Marilyn brought baked beans; and I made a cucumber and sour cream salad.

Galumphing Betty and the three goslings were peeking in the windows, so we had company for lunch. They then spent the afternoon playing with Marilyn's children and they all got along with only a few spats.

Dad did not want me to bring lunch or supper out, so I had packed two meals for him. The vicar helped him again after supper. Tonight, was ball practice, and he did not go. I guess several of the men came out to see why he would miss practice.

Wednesday, July 23, 1947

We sewed all day again, and the dresses are done. Mrs. Gehm came and sewed on buttons. Aunt Doris picked her up and took her home. She is so crippled up; it took both of us to help her into the car. I think she enjoyed being out and about.

Betty and the goslings were here for dinner and stayed to find out the latest adventures of Terry.

The oats are shattering, making thrashing go ever so slowly.

Thursday, July 24, 1947

I worked all day in both gardens. Dad thrashed all day and stored the oats in the granary. There will be plenty of feed for the animals next winter.

Friday, July 25, 1947

Well, the vicar told his teammates he would be helping Dad harvest oats and would not make it to tomorrow evening's game. After supper, four men showed up at the farm and helped get the rest of the oats done, so now he has no excuse to miss the game.

I was not sure what made Dad happier, to have the oats done or that the vicar is becoming part of the community.

He wondered aloud about the drinking that some of the teams do after the games.

Saturday, July 26, 1947

Dad worked on the machinery, oiling, and such so that it is ready for next week's spring wheat harvest.

He came home early. I was hoping he would rest, but he said he was going to Arlington to the ball game. What could I do but go along?

I had chicken fried steak ready, so I made sandwiches to eat as we drove.

Some of the men have started calling the vicar *lille Jakob.* He is far from little, over six foot and well built. Some are just calling him *Lille.* A strange young woman asked me who he was and remarked how handsome he was. I was glad he hit a home run at that moment, so we were distracted, and I did not have to answer. Of course, the De Smet Pioneers won!

Sunday, July 27, 1947

Dad and I drove to the North Preston church today. The vicar took his motorcycle and went to Huron for church and to talk to the priest there.

For dinner today I baked a meatloaf, fresh cucumber salad, tomatoes, mashed potatoes, and gravy.

Galumphing Betty and the little quails were here and joined us. They had to leave the house; they said their mother was sleeping.

The vicar came about supper time. Dad invited him to stay for cold sliced meatloaf and fresh garden vegetables.

Over tea, he told us that both the priests in Brookings and Huron have said that it seems so peculiar of the bishop. They both suggested that the vicar make another trip to Sioux Falls.

Then the talk turned to the baseball team and my leaving for Aberdeen.

We stayed up too late listening to the *Theatre Guild of the Air.* It was suspenseful.

Monday, July 28, 1947

I had trouble sleeping. I kept thinking of the story from the *Theater Guild.*

Dad started windrowing his spring wheat. I drove the tractor a few hours in the afternoon.

I had gone out to work in the garden, but the vicar keeps it weed free. There are a few cantaloupes that will be ripe soon.

While at the farm, I made us a supper of fried chicken, corn on the cob, tomatoes, and cucumbers.

Tuesday, July 29, 1947

We had a thunderstorm during the night that really drenched the wheat that is cut. It was too wet to windrow. It seems a bit unusual that the crops have ripened so quickly one after another.

Dad took five bushels of oats to the roller mill in Oldham. I don't know how we will eat five bushels of oatmeal. However, I am sure he will find someone to share it with.

Wednesday, July 30, 1947

I walked to town to get a few groceries, and Mrs. Speck was walking arm in arm with the bishop. He was again wearing a bowler. Even though they are so out of style, he looked quite dandy in it. I tried to get their attention, but they turned and hurried off in the other direction.

Thursday, July 31, 1947

Mrs. B. called and insisted that I come to see her. I really didn't want to. She finally asked me to bring her a cup of sugar. Once I was there, she asked me repeatedly about Mr. Warren. Did I find him good looking? Did I think he was intelligent? Did I look forward to spending time alone with him?

I wanted to tell her to mind her own business and stomp out. I also wanted to be kind, so I lied and told her I had bread rising and needed to get it in the oven.

On the way home, I ran into the bishop and Mrs. Speck. They tried to get away, but I was too fast and sneaky. I scurried around the block and up the alley, and there they were!

She did not introduce us, but I introduced myself and when I reached out to shake his hand, he turned my hand and kissed it. Oh my! He is a wormy fellow.

Friday, August 1, 1947

This morning before work, the vicar stopped by to tell me goodbye, and that I should enjoy my time in Aberdeen. He handed me a package. It was an elegant brown, marbled fountain pen. He lingered until I feared he would be late for work.

Mrs. B. was walking down the street singing that new song, "Smoke! Smoke! Smoke! That Cigarette." She would pretend to smoke and wriggle and sashay as she sang. When she saw me, she immediately stopped and tippity-tapped quickly past.

The De Smet Pioneers traveled to Huron for their game today. The vicar had to leave work early to get to the game on time. Dad talked about going, but he stayed home. He popped up a pan of popcorn, and we listened to *The Three Suns*.

* * * * *

Baum Boarding House
1900 Frank Str.
Aberdeen, So. Dak.
August 2, 1947

Dear Dad,

My train arrived in Aberdeen on time.

Thank you for the collection of Hawthorne's short stories. I wish I could say I read it on the trip. I was far too excited to concentrate and so enjoyed the scenery. I had a window seat, and the one next to me was empty, so I did not have to make conversation, and as a result I could relish the trip.

I was a bit bothered that you insisted I take a thermos of tea. However, I am glad you did, it only added to the pleasantness of the trip.

Someday I want to cross our great country with you. Oh, there is so much to see!

I asked for directions to the boarding house and started walking. But who should come along and offer to take our valise to our domicile?

Yes, you are correct, Mr. Warren.

Thank you for finding me such a comfortable place to stay. Mrs. Baum's is a spacious, clean, and pleasant place. The house must have housed a wealthy family at one time. There are two parlors and plenty of rooms and two stairways that lead up.

Mrs. Baum told me right away that I am to use the east stairs and never go on the men's side. If I were found up there, I would be turned out immediately. She then apologized and said that she in-formed all her guests of the same thing.

She looks so much like Almira Gulch from The Wizard of Oz, *it is uncanny.*

My room, which overlooks the back yard, is small, tidy, and pleasant. It has a bed, wardrobe, a dainty sewing rocker, and a desk. I will be most comfortable. From my window I can see a neat, well-tended vegetable and flower garden. The rows and spacing are very exact.

Supper was basic and filling. Mrs. Baum employs a cook and two young farm girls to help cook and clean.

There are twelve boarders, including myself. Of the five other women, four work in different offices at the college and one other is taking classes. The men are young professors from the college or work downtown at various jobs. One works in a law office.

A great deal of flirting and teasing goes on. I am sure I will be entertained.

After supper, a group walked to the park to listen to a band. It was warm, and the bugs were out with a vengeance. However, it was nice to do something besides sit in my room missing and worry-ing about you.

How is the vicar?

I am going to read a bit and then rest. I will probably write again tomorrow.

Thank you again for this break and opportunity.

Much love,

Hanna

P. S. When Mr. Anderson comes, would you ask him if he has a secondhand typewriter for sale? I can use the typewriters at the student union, but it would be nice to have one of my own. It will take quite a bit to get used to typing again.

Much Love,

Your,

Hanna

* * * * *

Sunday, August 3, 1947

The day loomed large before me. After breakfast, I walked to the closest Lutheran church. After lunch, the others asked me to join in their fun, which kept me busy for the rest of the day.

It makes me feel a bit odd, after we are served our meals, Mrs. Baum, her staff and her son, Harold, eat in the kitchen.

I am too excited to sleep; *I start classes tomorrow!*

* * * * *

Dear Miss. Morland,

I was walking by your house and your old dad was sitting on the porch writing. He said that he was writing you a letter and I could add one. So, I am.

How are you? I am fine. What are you doing? Did you like the train ride? I miss you. Do you miss me?

I better go.

your friend,

Betty

* * * * *

305 Second Str.

De Smet, So. Dak.

August 3, 1947

Dear Hanna,

I really do not have any news, but I wanted you to have a letter. Everything is fine here. Julia arrived on the late train yesterday and is most excited to be taking care of her older brother. I think I will be spending more time at the farm than before. Her constant chatter is already getting on my nerves.

Jacob did not come to church with us today. He left early on his motorcycle to visit with the priest at the church in Brookings.

The plans for the new church building are moving forward. I am sure you have noticed I am not in support of them. I think that I will soon need to find a new church home. It pains me to say that, but I cannot be a part of this.

Do not worry, I am in good hands. All the work will get done.

Enjoy yourself. If any of the other boarders ask you out, please go with my blessing. You need to spend more time with young people.

As I said, do not worry. But I do need to tell you that Mrs. B. came by this afternoon and she and Julia had their heads together. One wonders what evil intentions lurk in their minds. Ha!

Dad

* * * * *

Monday, August 4, 1947

I was up early and eager to attend my classes. In the morning, I will be attending lectures on the Primary Classroom, and will have several papers to write. I hope I can do as well as my fellow students; they seem so much more competent. I ate lunch in the cafeteria, rested outside on the beautiful campus and then went to my afternoon class, Diagnosing Reading Difficulties. Both professors are women and quite knowledgeable. I know I will learn a lot.

I read in the library until supper, went to my room and read some more. I hope I can keep up with my assignments.

The other boarders sat around in the parlor and talked. I would have liked to join them, but I needed to study.

There is one in particular that I would like to get to know better, Andrew. He is older than the rest; he was an airman, dark hair, and blue eyes. But I am not here to meet men.

* * * * *

Bishop J. Bradbury
Calvary Cathedral
Sioux Falls, South Dakota
August 4, 1947

Jacob Stewart
General Delivery
De Smet, South Dakota

Jacob Stewart,
I have not been to De Smet on July 16 or July 30 or any other
days.
I was in De Smet, as witnessed by my secretary on June 30. You
are very confused. All further correspondence from you will be de-
stroyed. Do not write to me.

His Holiness
Bishop Bradbury

* * * * *

Tuesday, August 5, 1947

From my window, I can see Mrs. Baum's son, Harold, come and go to work. He is quiet and spends his evenings tending his vegetable and flower garden or sitting on the back porch doing some handwork and listening to the radio. Andrew will sit on the back porch and talk to him, but otherwise Harold sticks to himself.

As we walked to class today, Janice took my hand and told me I had the hands of an old woman. She wants to show me how to care for my hands and paint my nails. She said she has a lovely shade of green that will compliment my hair.

After school, I stopped at the drug store and bought some Bag Balm, cotton socks, and hand cream. But no polish!

Mr. Warren seeks me out, every day, in the cafeteria.

Today was the meeting of the De Smet Ladies' Book Club. I wondered what was served and if they talked about the book. Aunt Julia was guaranteed to go.

* * * * *

305 2nd Str.
De Smet, So. Dak.
August 5, 1947

Hanna,

I am done harvesting spring wheat. It is all hauled to town and sold. The field work is all caught up. I have been helping Aunt Julia in the kitchen. She says it is just like old times and seems to be enjoying it. I spend a lot of time at the farm to get away from her jammering.

Jacob stopped in on Sunday evening and told me about his visit to Brookings. The priest there said all that has happened is so unlike Bishop Bradbury. Jacob did say that this Reverend Howard seems as if he could be a good friend.

Rev. Howard suggested again that Jacob make another trip to Sioux Falls. I am not certain why Jacob is so reluctant to make that trip.

The calico cat showed up with six kittens.
I miss you,
Dad

* * * * *

Wednesday, August 6, 1947

Before bed, I rubbed Bag Balm on my hands and wore cotton socks to bed. In the morning they were lying against the wall where I must have thrown them.

Yesterday, I could not decide which hand cream to buy, Softskin or Yardley. The clerk said Softskin was the best. However, I thought it smelled like an old lady, so I chose Yardley, which smelled of lavender.

At breakfast, I went into the dining room, and right away Janice noticed the scent. She remarked, "You smell like a hospital. You should try Softskin; it smells so flowery and pleasant."

I was trying to ignore her when Andrew spoke up and said he thought it gave a fresh and clean impression, such as a hay field. The discussion ended, but I could have crawled under the linoleum. I had put on just enough to cover my hands; I was not wearing the whole jar.

Thursday, August 7, 1947

Mr. Warren stopped by to visit after supper. We sat in the front parlor under the eagle eye of Mrs. Baum. I was glad she was there. Not that I would have allowed anything to happen, but it made him uncomfortable, which caused him to leave early. He left a book on the table. As I picked it up, a letter fell out. I saw it was from Mrs. B.

I would like to say I replaced it and did not read it, but after a few minutes of struggling, I read it.

* * * * *

Mrs. Arnold Balister
602 Second Street
De Smet, South Dakota
August 7, 1947

My dear Mr. Warren,

It was most delightful to see you while you were in De Smet last weekend. I am so glad that Hannah has decided to attend summer school <u>with</u> you.

She is just like a daughter to me. You must realize I was a very young teacher when I had her in the fourth grade. She was quite a know-it-all at that time and liked to show off her knowledge of the times tables. She thought she knew them better than me, but I only gave the wrong answers to quiz the children. I do know my multiplication tables.

She has really grown up, although she will never be as beautiful as her mother. Growing up, her mother and I were often told we would look like identical twins if her mother had beautiful black hair instead of red. And she was a wee bit taller than I am.

As I said, I have known her all her life. Her mother and I were quite close. Hannah's father has proposed to me several times. I have also received several proposals from a certain rich farmer whose initials are MW. He wants my money. I am not certain I am ready to marry again.

Hannah often confides in me. I know I have become a mother figure to her, and we share many secrets.

We often borrow from each other. Just this last week she bor-
rowed some vanilla from me.

Before she left, she called and wanted to come to my house for
tea. She told me she was looking forward to these classes and spend-
ing time with you. She did not say you specifically, but who else
could she mean? After all, she does think you are handsome, have a
strong singing voice, and are so intelligent.

I am sure you two will find a mutual admiration for each other.

Sincerely,
Lisa Balister

* * * * *

Friday, August 8, 1947

A whole week of school! I have learned so much.

After supper, Andrew asked if I would like to go to the concert at the band-shell. It was a bit of a walk, so we took the streetcar; he paid for my fare. We visited as we rode the trolley, and afterward while eating ice cream. He told me a bit about his time in the air corps and that he is an assistant professor of science.

* * * * *

Marilyn Koenig
Rural Route 4
De Smet, South Dakota
August 8, 1947

Hanna,

You have only been gone for a week, and I miss you. I have not
received enough letters from you. I would like to know more about
your classes and all that you are experiencing.

To think! You are the first of The Girls to go to college. I still
dream of taking classes once the children are grown. I still don't
know what I want to study, I just want to study.

Last evening, during the ball game, something very strange hap-
pened. Schultzie drove up in his old flivver and made it backfire sev-

eral times. I don't know why he needs to do that. But he does and everyone turns and looks.

The first time that it backfired, Jacob grabbed Stanley and dragged him over to the side and they lay in the dirt. Your dad was there and ran over immediately and talked to Jacob. Slowly, Jacob sat up and released Stan.

Schultzie had also run over and kept apologizing, but your dad told him to "shut up and go away" (I never thought I'd hear your dad talk that way).

It took forever or about thirty minutes, and Jacob returned to himself. He sat on the sidelines the rest of the game.

We have been sewing up a storm at our house. New school dresses for my girls. And canning. I hope I never see another cob of corn. And did I say canning. Haha!

I miss you, girl.

Marilyn

* * * * *

Saturday, August 9, 1947

This week passed so quickly. Mrs. Baum allowed me to use her laundry tubs. I was allowed to use the ringer but not the agitator tub. The others must send out their laundry.

Janice said she had never done laundry, so I helped her. Really, she stood and watched as I washed her clothes. She was amazed that one could do it without an agitator tub.

Then everything needed to be ironed. I showed Janice how and left her alone with the iron.

She talked the whole time we were together. Janice teaches in a small school outside of Wagner. She said it was stifling and she was going to get her degree so she could teach in a larger school and escape small town life. Janice told me the school board reminded her twice that it says in her contract she is not to get pregnant during the school year. Preggers as she put it. She wishes she could move to the west coast, because there are more jobs available to women out there.

She also told me of an automatic washing machine that converts to a dishwasher which she had seen in *Life* magazine. She thinks that someday every home will have one. I am not sure I want to wash my undergarments in the same machine that I wash dishes with, although one of those automatic washers would be nice. I am thankful to at least have an agitator tub at home.

Andrew was late for lunch and came in with an armload of books. Mrs. Baum gave him a disgusted look and said, "I see you have been to the Jew again. If you keep bringing home books, you will be doing your own dusting."

Eileen then whispered to me that each Saturday he goes to a secondhand store and buys books, and every week she yells at him. He just smiles at her and gets away with murder.

When we were leaving the dining room, I asked him where the store was. He said he would take me, but he could not shield me from the wrath of Mrs. Baum.

Kaufmann's Secondhand Store is only a few blocks east of downtown. It was a treasure trove of junk. There was an old spinning wheel, toys, clothes, dishes, and books. Books! Shelf after shelf of books. I limited myself to just a few children's books.

When we got back to the boarding house, Mrs. Baum glared and said, "Now don't you lead that young woman astray."

Andrew just laughed and whispered to me, "Her bark is far worse than her bite."

When I was on the side porch reading, Andrew joined me, and we read until it was too dark. Mrs. Baum strictly forbids anyone to be in the kitchen, but Andrew snuck in and took some cookies and a bottle of milk. We enjoyed our ill-gotten gains. Something tells me she knows he helps himself to cookies and milk but turns a blind eye.

Sunday, August 10, 1947

I walked to the closest Lutheran church. The Baums were there, so I sat with them, and they offered me a ride home.

I had wanted to study all afternoon.

Mr. Warren called after dinner. Andrew and I were sitting on the porch, and I felt so low. Andrew's face fell when Mr. Warren arrived; he shortly excused himself and went inside. Mr. Warren insisted that while we are in Aberdeen, we are to call us William. He asked me to go for a walk, but I declined.

Janice came out and introduced herself and gushed all over him. She insisted he take her for a walk. They left with her arm entwined in his.

* * * * *

Dear Miss Morland,

Your old dad was again on the porch. I wanted to talk to you, but you are still gone. I had a bad week. I was hoping to get a book to read. I like the book about that doll named Hitty. I like dolls. Do you like dolls?

Mama told us to stay in the house, but Lily went out. I got a whoopin' for letting her go out. I am sorry that I am so bad. I try so hard to be good. What can I do to make Lily stay in?

I do not like it when Mama is mad, she calls me gimp and crip. That is mean like dirt.

I miss you.

your friend,
Betty

longer letter later

* * * * *

Ernst Morland
305 2nd Str.
De Smet, So. Dak.
August 10, 1947

Dear Hanna,

Your Aunt Julia and I went to church, came home, ate dinner, and then we went walking and stopped in to see a few of the old neighbors.

Jacob again went on his motorbike and visited with the Episcopalian priest in Huron. He was here for supper. Julia did offer to do his laundry, but he said he was fine.

Yesterday he borrowed our mower, and he and Bob Gates mowed the lawn at St. Stephen's. He said it was hard to see the church fall into disrepair again.

Everything on the farm is going well. We had quite a south wind on Thursday, so I brought all the windfalls in for Julia to make applesauce. I also culled the old hens and sold most of them to Peschl's. I kept and butchered a dozen, so Julia canned them. I am trying to keep her busy.

She is not so busy that she does not have time to talk. Mrs. B. is here almost every day to visit. Obviously, if she has so much time to talk to Mrs. B., I am not keeping her busy enough.

I suggested to her that you would really appreciate it if she would wash the windows while she is here. But it will be just my luck; she will fall off the ladder and spend six months here recuperating.

Betty and her sisters come almost every day. They want to listen to their radio program. Julia makes them sit on the back porch and listen to the radio through the window. She did have me move it closer to the window so that they could hear better.

She removed all the cushions from the porch furniture. After sunning them and beating them furiously, she stored them in the attic. She guaranteed that not a single louse remained alive, if there ever were any.

When I suggested she feed the girls something every day, she harrumphed a few times, but has given them food. I should add an adverb in there. She loudly harrumphed, a few times. And mumbled something about feeding them will send me to the poor house. I might as well sell the farm and just move to the poor house. Ha!

So, life continues. I miss you and hope you are enjoying yourself.
Much love,
Dad

P. S. Pray for Jacob. I am beginning to see why the Lord put him in my path and heart.

* * * * *

Monday, August 11, 1947

Today in reading class we had a lively discussion on sight reading versus phonics. I have decided I need to emphasize phonics more. Mrs. Sollig gave me a book with rhymes for each sound. I think I will have the children learn the rhymes after our opening exercises.

Mr. Warren, we mean William, met me as I was walking to lunch. He walked me to the dining hall and sat with me.

I decided I needed to be most truthful. I tried, but I just could not get it out. I fear that with all my bumbling, Mr. Warren thinks the opposite of what I want him to.

When I got to the boarding house, Andrew was on the front porch reading. He looked up, said hello, and returned to his reading. Feeling quite awkward, I went in and up to my room.

I studied and worked on my paper until I could not keep my eyes open and then sleep did not come.

Tuesday, August 12, 1947

Mr. Warren was at the boarding house this morning wanting to walk me to school. I was so glad when Janice and Eileen came out at about the same time. Janice walked up to him and slid her hand through his arm; then they walked ahead, arm in arm. Eileen and I walked behind.

Janice asked him to come after supper and explain something from the class she is taking.

After supper, I saw Mr. Warren come up the walk, so I made a hasty exit and sat on the back porch with Andrew, Jack, and Harold as they listened to the radio.

* * * * *

Miss H. Morland
Baum Boarding House
1900 Frank Str.
Aberdeen, South Dakota
August 12, 1947

Dear Betty,

Thank you so much for your letters. I have so enjoyed hearing from you. I am sorry that you have had some difficult days.

You are most welcome to borrow any of my books, which you wish. My "old" dad can help you get them. (I am not sure he would like it if he knew you called him old.) Yes, I liked Hitty. Yes, I like dolls. Ask Dad if you could find a book called Understood Betsy. *It may be a bit hard for you, but I do think you will like it.*

I am sure your mother does not mean to hurt you when she calls you names. She is just angry and speaking without thinking. That is why I want you to read Understood Betsy; *the adults in the book think they understand Betsy best. In the end, they find they do not really understand.*

I hope you are enjoying the warm weather.

Yes, I did like the train ride. Have you ever ridden a train?

I am living in a large house with a kind lady and many other young people.

Yes, I am enjoying my classes. I hope this will make me a better teacher.

What silly things have the little girls been up to? I can only imagine.

Please write to me soon.

Your friend,
Miss Morland

* * * * *

Wednesday, August 13, 1947

The weather has been so hot; it is difficult to concentrate. Last night I slept on the east porch. After breakfast, Mrs. Baum took me aside and told me I should not do that alone.

Poor Mrs. Baum, neither of her hired girls showed up this morning. They called and said they would be going back to the farm and getting married. Harriet, the cook, was furiously slinging out breakfast, mumbling and fussing the whole time.

After breakfast, Andrew marched into the kitchen and started doing the dishes. Harriet stood akimbo and asked him just what he thought he was doing. He said he was going to wash, and I was going to dry. I quickly joined him. He then got all the others to help clear the table, scrape the dishes, and help wash and dry. We all then hurried to school and work.

I went to the kitchen after school and helped get supper on. And again, after supper, Andrew got everyone working, even Janice.

When we were on the porch reading, after supper, Andrew whispered he had not told anyone else this, but did I not think Mrs. Baum looked like Almira Gulch? I replied I had thought that the first time I saw her. It sent us laughing. I could not look at him or her without giggling all evening.

Thursday, August 14, 1947

KP Duty (as Andrew called it) again for everyone. Harriet did seem to enjoy the help and was in a better mood today.

Mrs. Baum looks very tired. It will be a blessing when she gets some help.

Friday, August 15, 1947

There is something special and commanding about Andrew. He gets everyone, even Janice, to work after every meal, and they all seem to enjoy it.

Mrs. Baum said she has new girls starting this coming Monday.

Saturday, August 16, 1947

I did laundry this morning. As I was taking the clothes off the line, Harold came over to talk to me. He is going to share some of his zinnia seeds with me.

In the afternoon, Andrew and I walked again to Kaufmann's. I could not resist buying a complete set of O. Henry's short stories. Andrew and I talked about Mr. Kaufmann. I had never met a Jew before, and he seems like such a kind and generous man. Andrew said many of Mr. Kaufmann's family died in concentration camps.

After that, I studied. Then in the evening, we all went to a dance at a hall on Main Street. It was a bit of a walk, and I could see Andrew was tired when we arrived. He did not dance much, or I should say, we did not dance much. He did ask me to waltz with him.

* * * * *

Betty Jane Speck
De Smet, South Dakota

Dear Miss. Morland,

I got your letter and went right away to your old dad and asked if he would let me have a stamp and all to write to you. He is so nice.

It is hot. We have had to stay inside a lot; Mama is busy at the hotel. She has had to spend the nights there a few times as they do not have anyone to run the hotel at night.

Mama works so hard. I want to make life easier for her, but I am so bad, and the girls do not mind me.

Your old dad loaned me the Betsy book. It is hard for me to read, but I like it.

U R 2 good to B 4gotten
Betty Jane Speck

* * * * *

Sunday, August 17, 1947

St. Mark's Episcopal Church is only a block further than the Lutheran church, so I decided to go there today. It was a different service than what we had attended with the vicar at St. Stephen's. The organ music was inspiring.

Mr. Warren called after dinner, but Janice whisked him off to one of the porches, so I did not have to talk to him.

She is quite taken by him. She says he may be her ticket out of South Dakota. When she told me that, I had a sudden tinge of jealousy, but it quickly gave way to complete relief. She may have him.

Monday, August 18, 1947

The new girls started working today, so we are off KP duty. On the table, in my room, was a lovely bouquet of zinnias. None of the other girls got one. I assume it is from Mrs. Baum.

* * * * *

August 18, 1947

Dear Miss. Morland,

This morning mama told us a bus was coming to town. She gave us each five cents to spend. We went to the courthouse, and there was an old, rickety, school bus. It did not look like much until we got inside. It was a store! It was hard for me to keep the girls out of stuff. The boss of the bus gave us mean looks. Your old dad came in and helped me with the girls. He gave us each another nickel. It was hard to know what to spend it on. I got five penny dolls and a notebook, and some pencils and the mean man gave me a wonderful little thing. You stick your pencil in it and when you turn the pencil it comes out all sharp. Your dad said to be careful and not sharpen my pencils all away to nothing. He is so smart.

The mean man turned out to be not as mean as his face. He pulled two cigar boxes out of the cupboard and told me to put everything in them. I am going to make one into a little house for my new dolls and keep my pencils in the other one.

Just as we were about to leave, your old aunt walked in and gave us each another nickel. Do you know that makes fifteen cents? I bought mama three new handkerchiefs, plus two for each of the girls, and one for me.

Your old aunt was looking at fabric and asked us what we liked. Every time the man would tell her a price, she would look mean at him. He then would look mean back. It was like a contest to see who could look meaner. He was getting out some shoes, and she said, "Put them away who needs your old shoes?"

She told us to go, and so we did.

Miss. Morland, it was such a magical bus, I am sorry you missed it. Do you have magical buses way up in Aberdeen where you are?

I miss you.

Your friend,
Betty

* * * * *

Betty Speck
102 Calumet No. East
De Smet, South Dakota
August 19, 1947

Dear Miss. Morland

Your old dad gave me some more paper and stamps. I forgot to tell you this yesterday. In the back of the bus was a lady. She looked old and young at the same time. She had brown hair pulled back in a braid. Her eyes were slanty like a Chinaman. She was working away at some strips of cloth with a hook. As soon as she saw your old dad, she plunked on a hat with cherries and daisies that bobbled and waved as she walked. She took his hand and said to the boss of the bus "Bye Dad, I go see Hanna."

He had to tell her a few times that you were not home. She seemed very sad. But she went back and kept hooking. When I got back that far, she looked at me and said, "Hanna my friend."

Who is she? Why does she look like an old lady and a little girl at the same time? What does she do with all her hooking?

Your friend,
Betty

* * * * *

Wednesday, August 20, 1947
When I came home from school, there was another fresh bouquet of zinnias. In front of the vase was a clever little box made from post cards that were sewn together with intricate stitches.

* * * * *

Hanna Morland
1900 Frank Str.
Aberdeen, So. Dak
August 21, 1947

Dear Dad,
Today was a hard day. I thought of you often and wondered why I was so far from home and not at home where I belong.

It has been hot, but today seemed unbearably hot. I went to class and studied. I felt like a machine, just making the motions.

I wish that we could sit on the porch with a cup of tea and talk.

I miss Mom. I thought of how always when we came home from school, she would have a glass of milk and some sort of snack ready and waiting. We would burst in and joyously hug her and run for the table. Her eyes were so bright in those days. She sat with us and talked about our day. Clucking like a hen when we said anything she thought disagreeable.

I well remember, in fourth grade, when I was sent home with lice. I walked in the door wailing and pulling on my braids. Mom hugged me and gave me milk and cookies. Oh, then the odorous lice treatment. First, she poured kerosene all over my head and worked it in. She rubbed with her fingernails; I thought she would rub my scalp off. All the while she continued to talk lightly, and before long it was bearable. Then came the lye soap and hot rinses and fine combing it out.

I returned to school the next day only to find out more children had also been sent home. It was not long until everyone in the class was sent home.

She did this dreaded treatment every third day for two weeks. By the end of the first week, I almost looked forward to that time with Mom. She could make any difficult task seem bearable.

Even though today was most difficult, and we have had other difficult times, we have so much to be thankful for. We have each other. We are surrounded by family and friends that love us and care for us. But you know that.

I missed you a lot today and wished I could give you a hug.

So dear Dad, I hope that the many good memories warmed your heart. I miss her too.

Much love,
Your,
Hanna

* * * * *

Jacob Stewart
General Delivery
De Smet, South Dakota
August 21, 1947

Dear Mother,

I trust you had a good day and are well rested. I hope that the city is not too hot this year and you have a respite from the heat.

I have been remembering the times we went to Rock Away Beach to escape the heat of the city. Dad so enjoyed the beach and swimming.

After supper, I took a walk in the pasture and had a feeling to visit Ernst in town. I ignored it. But when I got back to the house from my walk, he was sitting alone on the porch. I made a cup of coffee for him. We talked about the weather and crops.

All of sudden, he began talking of his wife. It was two years ago today that she died. He told me of his son, David, dying on Normandy Beach and how after that his wife gave up. She slowly died until one day he came home from the farm and found her resting in the arms of Jesus.

Our talk went to the first war. Mr. Morland had stayed home, and his older brother had gone, only to return a different man. For the rest of his life, he was plagued with dreams and rarely slept. Edvard never married and was drafted again in the last war. Although he applied for a deferment, the local draft board, led by a neighbor, Melvin Wiese, did not grant him CO status, so he the spent the war in jail. He came home, only to die.

To lose three family members to war seems overwhelming. I could only sit and listen. At one point, when he was overcome with tears, I put my arms around him.

He has so often comforted and listened to me. I could only do the same. I offered my meager prayers.

We then went into the house for more coffee and continued talking until early morning.

Mother, please pray for this family.

I remain,

Your loving son,

Jacob

* * * * *

Hanna

in Aberdeen but wanting to come home

August 22

Marilyn! Where are you when I need you the most!

After class, I came back to the boarding house and who was in the entry way waiting for me? No, do not bother to guess. I will tell you. MELVIN WIESE, that's who! He was in town and wondered if I wanted to go to dinner. I excused myself to my room and said that I would return shortly. Mrs. Baum met me in the upper hall and glared at me. I explained that he was a neighbor from home.

I did not want to go to dinner with him. But I did. I ate really fast. I could hardly choke down the food. I tried not to prolong any conversation. It was awful. He must have run out of things to say about himself, so then he took me home.

It gets worse!

He walked me to the door and stumbled around. Did he want to kiss me?

I quickly went in and made a mad dash to my room.

Why are you so far away?

It gets even more worse!

I barely got into my room when Evelyn, one of the women boarders, barged in. She was mad! She went into a long tirade.

"You! You! It is women like you that make life miserable for other women. You come here with your country ways and try to get the attention of every man and then you have these rich farmers come calling on you. You are not content with one man, but you think you must have them all. Why don't you just go back home where you belong?"

She stomped out and slammed the door. I threw myself on my bed and cried. Eileen came in and tried to soothe my hurt feelings. She is a dear, but she is not you.

Eileen said that Evelyn has a big crush on Andrew and on Harold. What does that have to do with me?

I was hungry, so I went downstairs to see if there was any bread in the dining room. Andrew and Evelyn were in there talking; she stomped upstairs as soon as I walked in.

Andrew went into the kitchen and found me some milk and date nut bread. We went to the side porch, and he told me he heard her yelling through the walls and that not everyone thought as she did.

I am coming home. I will leave on the morning train and come home.

Hanna

P. S. It is morning. I am still embarrassed. But going to hold my head up and move forward som en god norsk jente. *(Like a good Norwegian girl. When are you ever going to learn Norwegian?)*
HKM

Saturday, August 23, 1947

The heat was oppressive. The girls and I took our blankets and pillows and slept outside on the upper balcony.

After breakfast, Andrew and I walked to Kaufmann's, and we both bought more books. Mr. Kaufmann gave me two peach crates. I am going to ask Dad to make a bookshelf for me with them.

I went to the student union and used the typewriters. I had to wait until there was a free one.

Then, I found the shadiest spot outdoors and studied. After supper, Janice, Eileen, and I walked to the drug store and had ice cream. I got a chocolate egg cream.

* * * * *

Hanna Morland
Aberdeen, South Dakota
August 23, 1947

Dear Betty,

I am so glad you liked the bus. When I was your age, I too thought it was magical.

The Anderson family travels around to small towns and sells and buys all sorts of things. When I was a girl and wanted something, Dad would say, "Wait until the Andersons come."

Mr. Anderson's father used to come to De Smet. He is older now and does not travel on the bus any longer. He had even meaner looks than his son. You will learn that they both have a heart of gold.

I am also so glad you met my friend Peggy. Peggy's mother died when she was young, so she travels with her dad. She sits in the back of the bus and crochets many beautiful rugs for them to sell. She knows just what colors will look good together.

Peggy is a Mongoloid. Many Mongoloids live in a hospital in Redfield, but Peggy's dad has kept her at home.

Mongoloid—I do not like that name. Just as you do not like being called gimp or crip. Peggy was born thinking differently than others. I think of her as just my friend Peggy. As you are just my friend Betty, and that is enough. You are you and Peggy is Peggy, and I am Hanna.

I am so surprised she is still wearing that hat. It was my Aunt Brigitta's best Sunday hat. When she died, I sold it to Mr. Anderson. As I was carrying it on the bus, Peggy saw it and claimed it as hers. It looks better on Peggy than it did on my aunt.

I hope you are continuing to read and taking good care of those silly sisters of yours.

Continue being a good girl, I will be home soon, and we will have so much to talk about over a cup of tea.

Your friend,
Miss Morland

* * * * *

Miss Morland,

Today as the girls and I walked past the depot, I saw the preacher picking weeds in a flower garden. I stopped and helped. The Depot Boss brought out a chair and watched us. The girls watched too. He is a good worker. The preacher not the boss. He gave us each a bottle of pop. The boss not the preacher.

Your friend,
Betty Jane Speck

* * * * *

Sunday, August 24, 1947

Mrs. Baum's family was here for the day. They all live in the area and came for her birthday. I felt badly that I did not know and at least have a card for her. Evelyn, who has lived here the longest knew and she had us each sign a card and give money. Mrs. Baum has been so kind to me that I gave her a whole dollar.

I was the only boarder invited to eat with her family. I was seated next to Harold, who is quiet, but made an effort to visit. He is good looking in a squarish, reliable, German sort of way. Harold has started his own construction business; his hands are strong, and work worn.

After supper, Andrew was sitting on the side porch reading. I joined him, but we did not talk more than to say hello.

H. K. M.
1900 Frank Str.
Aberdeen, So. Dak.

Dear Marilyn,

I am sorry I have not written to you very often since beginning this adventure.

I will have so much to tell you when I get home. We will have to go off to the lake and spend the day talking.

Please go to my room in the bottom drawer of my small dresser is a white, lawn handkerchief with off white lace in the pineapple pattern. You may have seen me working on it last winter. Mail it to me as soon as you can. I need a small thank you gift for Mrs. Baum.

I would ask Dad, but he would look all day and not find it.

Hugs to you my sweet friend.

Hanna

* * * * *

Monday, August 25, 1947

This is my last week of school. I have two papers to type and the final tests to get ready for. Oh, I hope I pass!

* * * * *

August 25, 1947
General Delivery
De Smet, South Dakota

Dearest Mother,

So soon after the anniversary of Mr. Morland's wife's death he has suffered again. Please remember this family in your prayers.

The remains of their former neighbor and son's best friend were identified and returned home for burial. A sealed coffin arrived at the depot on Friday of last week. Shortly after it arrived the mortician came with the hearse, and we loaded it.

Ernst was very quiet all week. I did not press him to talk but made myself available. On Saturday after he had finished chores he was waiting for me on my back steps. I asked him to stay for supper, but he thought he should go home and eat with his sister. He then asked me to go to the funeral with him.

He had decided not to tell his daughter about the funeral; he did not want to disturb her time away at college. I did wonder at the wisdom of that but decided I should not interfere. He wants to go to Aberdeen next week, and bring her home. He will tell her then.

I arrived at the house, and he was waiting in the pickup. His sister was not happy; she rode with a friend since he told her she needed to find her own ride.

The funeral was at one of the country churches. The building and yard were full of people of all ages. There was a feeling of heaviness and relief. The family's sorrow was renewed as they remembered the life of Sargent Henry Norgaard. However, I believe they experienced relief knowing he was now home. As "Taps" was played and the coffin lowered into the gaping hole, most everyone was sobbing. Then someone started singing the hymn, "Children of the Heavenly Father" in Norwegian. The entire group joined in.

The lunch afterwards was a time of remembering. I felt a bit strange; the family specifically asked Mr. Morland to join them at their table and he grabbed me by the arm and took me along. The family and Mr. Morland reminisced about the escapades of their sons, and the many adventures they had growing up on farms near each other.

Mr. Morland asked me to drive home. On the way home, he began sobbing heavily. I drove out to Lake Thompson, and we sat there until he was composed enough to go home. I helped him with chores and then ate supper with him and his sister. She was very quiet, which is very unusual for her.

After supper we sat on the back porch and drank our tea. Neither of us talked. When I left to go home, he hugged me and thanked me.

Please keep them in your prayers. Pray that I will have the wisdom to find words of comfort for them.

Your loving son,
Jacob

* * * * *

E. Morland
305 2ⁿᵈ St.
De Smet, So. Dak.
Aug. 25, '47

Hanna,

I have decided I need to see where you are staying and the col-lege. I will drive up next Saturday and bring you safely home.

My motives are also a bit selfish. I will be away from your Aunt Julia and her constant haranguing for two days.

I am sure the trusty A will make it. I asked Jacob to accompany me, but he has a ballgame.

I miss you,
Dad

* * * * *

H. Morland
1900 Frank Street
Aberdeen, South Dakota
August 25, 1947

Mr. Anderson,

I came home from school, and in the entryway, a box was wait-ing for me. When she was out, Mrs. Baum, my landlady, picked it up from the depot. Thank you so much! The Remington typewriter is beautiful and works so smoothly. Her son unpacked it and told me it had been recently cleaned and oiled.

You also included extra ribbons. Thank you for being so thoughtful. You are always so kind to me.

After supper, I put it to good use and hammered out a paper for my class on teaching reading.

I am so sorry that I missed you when you were in De Smet. I hope you come our way again this autumn.

Please give Peggy a hug for me.

Sincerely,
Hanna Morland

Tuesday, August 26, 1947

After supper, Janice and I went to the movie, "The Bachelor and the Bobby Soxer." Cary Grant is so handsome. I do not like the way the movie ended.

Sitting in the air conditioning was a relief.

I then stayed up way too late studying.

Wednesday, August 27, 1947

Morning came way too soon. But I managed to get through classes and get my papers typed and ready to turn in tomorrow.

Mr. Warren came to see Janice. They sat on the front porch. Every time she called him Willie, I am not sure if he was grimacing or glowing.

Thursday, August 28, 1947

When I got up, there was a postcard from Harold Baum slid under my door. With neat, square printing, he asked me to write to him when I got home.

Mr. Warren met me outside the cafeteria.

"Miss. Morland, we need to talk. We must confess that we are very interested in another young woman. We cannot say what will come of this interest, but we are free to date others."

I thanked him for his candor. I told him I was confident we would continue to have a positive and pleasant working relationship. I would continue to respect him as my principal.

I hoped my relief and pleasure at his announcement, and the fact that I was lying did not show too much.

I know I was smiling as I walked home. Andrew caught up with me and said I was shining with happiness.

"We were told that we are free to date others," I replied.

His eyes twinkled, and he smiled as he replied, "We see."

I hope Andrew understood that I have not been going with Mr. Warren.

Friday, August 29, 1947

Final exams! Oh, my head still aches from all the thinking. When I thanked the professors and told them goodbye, they both encouraged me to continue studying.

When I got back to Mrs. Baum's, I knew something was up. Everyone was acting so nervous. Mrs. Baum had a cake, and there were little presents from everyone, except Evelyn and Andrew. Janice gave me a bright red scarf. They all wished me the best school year ever.

When I went upstairs, I found, on my table, a book, neatly wrapped in heavy, brown wrapping paper. It was a copy of William Wordsworth's poems, from Harold.

After supper, Janice came in while I was packing and said Andrew wanted to talk to me on the side porch.

Andrew was sitting there alone. He said he wanted to keep in touch, and would I be interested in exchanging letters? I was so surprised I could only nod.

He then told me he had a present for me in his room. He would like for me to go up to his room so that when I read his letters, I would picture him in his room. My heart was beating so wildly, I thought it would jump out of my chest. Again, I could only nod.

With Janice and Tom standing guard, we snuck up the west stairs. They sat near the steps and were supposed to break into song if Mrs. Baum came near.

Andrew's room was tidy and organized. There was a bed, wardrobe, comfortable looking Morris chair and footstool, a small table, a desk, and a bookshelf that was overflowing. On the walls and wardrobe were stuffed birds and small mammals of all sorts. There was a flower press spilling over with dried flowers and grasses. Since it is a corner room, it had three windows. It was large and comfortable.

He handed me a small package and asked me to open it later. Taking another quick look around the room to seal it in my memory, I made an immediate departure. I was halfway down the stairs when Janice and Tom started singing loudly!

Oh! Those two! Mrs. Baum was nowhere in sight. They laughed so hard, Janice had tears running down her cheeks, causing her make-up to avalanche down her face. They kept saying, "Your face! You should have seen your face."

Once alone, I opened the package. It was a souvenir china cup. It had a picture of Old Main and said, "Remember Me, Aberdeen, South Dakota."

Saturday, August 30, 1947

Dad arrived at 10 A.M. He left home at 6 A.M. and made good time. He said he often wondered if the pick-up would make the 125 miles. I was glad and sad that the vicar was not with him.

As I introduced him around, Janice latched onto his arm and said, "OHHH you didn't tell me he was so handsome." Dad blushed! I do not believe I have ever seen him blush. Even Mrs. B. cannot make him blush!

After meeting everyone, he took me to lunch at a diner downtown, and we toured the campus. I was so pleased to run into both professors. Dad, the old farmer, moved with comfortable ease in it all.

Then we did a bit of shopping. I talked Dad into a new pair of work boots and a suit. At Brown's Department Store, we found a beautiful ready to wear navy blue suit. The pants are a bit big, but I can alter them at home. I was fingering some fabric, and he walked up and said that it would make nice curtains for my bedroom.

That was exactly what I was thinking. Dad bought twelve yards. I told him I only needed eight, but he thought I would like to make some "doodads and gewgaws" out of the extra.

"And what precisely are doodads and gewgaws?"

"Chair covers, pillows, and other such girly things," was his answer.

At Woolworths, I found some jack sets and small cars for my-first graders for Christmas. There were three baby dolls and a set of Raggedy Ann books. I had to get those for Betty and Lily and Rose and Violet. I also had to get something for Marilyn's children. I ended up spending $7.00 just on the children.

Then on to Kaufmann's Secondhand Store. While I was looking at books, Dad and Mr. Kaufmann spoke in quite tones, and exchanged addresses. I found a larger baby doll that I had to buy for Betty. I think it will clean up nicely and I have plans for some clothes and a blanket.

And Dad and I talked. It was so good to hear all the news. Dad told me Aunt Doris and Marilyn had sewn three dresses each for Betty and the chickies. The vicar continues to work at the depot, and he has been visiting with different priests to see what can be done about his situation. Dad, who does not gossip, had lots of news for me.

For supper, we were back at Mrs. Baum's. Then Andrew walked with us to the band shell for a concert.

Sunday, August 31, 1947

After church and dinner, we were all packed to go.

I went back in to thank Mrs. Baum again, and give her the handkerchief, as I came out; I heard Andrew and Dad talking.

"I asked Hanna to write me."

"What did she say?"

"She said she would."

"Then she will. Good luck, young man. She is a funny girl; she does not realize that she has several suitors," Dad said.

I do know there are men interested, but it seems to be all the wrong ones.

We stopped on the roadside and ate the lunch that Mrs. Baum had sent along. We sat there a while before Dad finally said he had something to tell me. He was not sure he had done the right thing and if he had not, he hoped I would forgive him. Then, through tears, he told me of Henry Norgaard's body coming home and being buried. It seems so unreal. I could have taken the train down for the funeral, but I am not sure I could have returned to school and concentrated.

We sat for a long time and talked about the funeral, the boys, and Mom.

We arrived home at eight. Aunt Julia met us at the door, but as soon as we could, we quietly went our own ways, lost in our own thoughts.

* * * * *

Andrew O'Brien
1900 Frank Str.
Aberdeen, So. Dak
August 31, 1947

Dear Hanna,

You just left this afternoon and already I want to send you a letter.

I enjoyed getting to know you these past few weeks. Thank you for saying you would write to me.

How was your trip?

Did you see any exciting sights? I guess a trip across the South Dakota prairie may not be considered exciting; beautiful, but not exciting.

I too have a week off before school starts again. I was thinking of taking a motor trip to the Black Hills to see Mount Rushmore. I thought I would also do a little hiking.
What will you do on your week off?
I look forward to hearing from you.
Sincerely,
Andrew O'Brien

* * * * *

Monday, September 1, 1947
Labor Day

I have one week to get ready for school.

Betty and the little quails came to see me first thing in the morning. I was so glad to see them that I had to give them each two hugs. They, of course, had not eaten breakfast so I ate again with them.

Aunt Julia was not at all pleased when she walked into the kitchen and saw us eating off Mom's second best china. It was a special occasion.

Mrs. B. came to see Aunt Julia. She was madder than a hornet. On Saturday, she had taken the train to Huron to the State Fair. She waited all day in line at the women's building to see Wynn Speece, *Your Neighbor Lady.* And Wynn never showed up. There were no excuses and no explanations. She did not come to the State Fair as advertised. Aunt Julia said she had listened to her every day and that she never mentioned anything on her program about not coming.

There was a baseball tournament today at the local fairgrounds. De Smet Pioneers, De Smet Farmers, Lake Henry Outlaws, Willow Lake Pirates, Volga Boatmen, and Hetland Hustlers all played. The wives and families prepared a picnic supper for after the games. I made a roaster of baked beans.

Betty and the ducklings joined us to watch the games. Lily asked why they were calling the vicar *lille,* "He's name is not Lily, mine is." I explained that they were calling him *lille,* which is Norwegian for little. Betty then remarked, "There ain't nothin' little about him."

When the team joined us for supper, and I saw the vicar up close, I was tongue tied and stammered. He came to greet me and extended his hand to shake mine. I had a bowl in each hand and was so flustered that I just stood there and did not know what to do. He took the bowl from my right and took my right hand in his large rough one. He asked me about my time in Aberdeen and then slowly went back to the men.

He is even better looking than I remember. He is tanned and filled out. His shirt was wet with sweat and clung to him.

In the end, we came in third. The vicar played well; he hit a double and made several outs.

We celebrated the end of the baseball season. Schultzie brought a washtub full of beer. While some of the others drank, the vicar kept busy cranking ice cream.

Tuesday, September 2, 1947
Name Day for people named Lisa

What a day! I feel as if I have been in a windstorm. My emotions have been from one extreme to another.

Janice called me today to tell me that she was moving to De Smet! She has been offered a contract to teach fifth grade. She had trouble getting out of her contract at Wagner, but "Willie" had talked to the school board. She was wondering if she could stay with us until she found a place to board. What could I say? She was welcome anytime.

Immediately, I called Mrs. Poppen to see if she had a room. She does; so, I told her to save it for my friend.

Aunt Julia and I made a basket of gifts for Mrs. B's name day. I did not tell Aunt Julia that Mrs. B. had made fun of Name Days and called them foreign. But I did ask her to help me surprise Mrs. B. We had a tin of tea, some *pepperkake,* and a crocheted doily. She acted quite pleased with it all. I wanted to remind her of what she had said about Name Days, but I decided to be kind.

Afterward, I walked to the farm to gather, clean, and sort eggs. There were too many eggs to carry by myself so I will have to have someone take them to the station for me. Aunt Julia had recently been out and cleaned the summer kitchen, so it was still tidy.

I do not feel ready to move back into normal life.

In the afternoon, I walked out to the cemetery to see Henry's grave. I was glad for the three miles, so I had time to think. It seems unreal. The grave was like a giant wound in the earth. Grief took my breath away. I felt as if I were drowning.

I sat there and thought of all the fun we had growing up, me running after my big brother and his friend, the mud fights at the creek, snowball fights and ice fishing. Next to Marilyn and David, Henry was my best friend. I remembered the senior formal, after Duane decided to go with Paula. Henry was away at school, but he called from Brookings and asked if he could go with me. I laughed at how, when he took me home, we stood awkwardly at the door. Turning beet red, he patted me on the head, said "goodbye old top," turned, and whistled a tune as he walked to his car.

I remembered how after the attack on Pearl Harbor he and David signed up. Coming home on leave, he was so proud of his uniform. We walked along Lake Thompson. He declared that he had loved me since grade school and asked me to write to him every day. A promise I kept.

As I was preparing to leave the cemetery his mother and sister, Louise, drove in. I stayed and we hugged and talked and cried, and that made his leaving very real. How hard this must be on his family.

Oh, *how* I miss them. Mom, David, Uncle Edvard, and Henry.

At supper, Aunt Julia announced she has decided to stay long enough to attend the De Smet Ladies' Book Club next week. Dad gulped his tea and said, "Julia, you are most welcome to stay, but surely you want to get home to the peace and quiet of your own home. Your family needs you."

"No. One thing I need to do yet is to go through Edvard's things. I noticed that they are boxed up in the west room at the farm."

"I have not been ready to do that. Please leave it to me," Dad replied.

"No, we shall do it together."

Dad then excused himself and left the table. He went out the front door, and I did not see or hear him until late. As he left the table, Aunt Julia looked at me and whispered, "These things are best met straight on."

She then turned on me and said, "Lisa and I have been talking. We decided it is time you quit mooning over Henry. Now that you know he is gone, you can move on with your life and find someone, like that handsome principal or Melvin; both would be excellent catches for you."

I wish that I could have thought of something to say. I only stood there with my mouth agape, thinking unkind thoughts, and wanting to throw something at her.

I am not entirely sure what my feelings are for Henry. They are a mixture of older brother's best friend and first, schoolgirl crush. But I am most certain I have not been mooning over him. I mourn his loss, but I am confident God has something planned for me.

I wonder where Aunt Julia and Mrs. B. get their ideas.

Wednesday, September 3, 1947

Aunt Julia was ready to go to the farm with dad. He looked her square in the eye and said, "Julia, you are welcome to come to the farm. You are not going through Edvard's things. I am not ready for that. If you want to go through his clothes and take a sweater or something, you may. I was going to see if Mr. Anderson wanted to buy his clothes, but I was not ready when he was here. I am now. You may have his Bible if you wish. That is all that will be done. I am not quite sure what your motives are. You did not speak to him for the last six years. Then at the funeral, you wailed and carried on until you were an embarrassment."

"I saw that all his journals are packed in one box. I am taking them home to read."

"Julia do not make this into a huge issue. You are not reading his journals; I am not even sure I ever will. I think they should be burned. You may have any of his clothes and his Bible. If you want to go through the kitchen and take anything that was Mother's, you are also welcome. The rest will remain boxed up until I know what to do with it. Please do not end our visit on a sour note."

Her mouth was clamped shut tightly and her eyes blazed a steely blue ready for a fight. But it did not go any further. She realized she had finally pushed Dad as far as he would go.

I never understood why she refused to speak to Uncle Edvard after he was drafted and applied for conscientious objector status. When I asked Dad about it, all he said is that Edvard had seen enough death in the Great War. Aunt Julia felt it was a black mark on the family that he did not want to fight again.

I went to the De Smet Hotel to talk to Mrs. Speck. But she was not around. I still wonder how she keeps her job.

There was an oily shoe salesman in the lobby that greeted me. He came over and stood too close. He smelled of hair grease, cigarettes, and liquor. He asked me if he could come over later and show me his samples. I told him I was too busy and not at all interested. I left as soon as I could.

Mrs. B. stopped in to see Aunt Julia, telling us she called the WNAX office in Yankton and gave them a piece of her mind about missing Wynn Speece. They told her Wynn had missed a few days of work to have a baby, and that she named her Gretchen. To make up for her inconvenience, they are mailing her a 1945 and a 1946 cookbook.

Autumn

Thursday, September 4, 1947

Janice arrived on the morning train, with boxes and trunks and bags and suitcases. The vicar said he would deliver it all later. I asked him if it could stay at the depot until she found a permanent place to stay. I walked her to the school and showed her around.

Leaving her in the capable hands of Mr. Warren, I settled into working in my room.

On the way home, we stopped at Mrs. Poppen's. Janice thinks she will be comfortable there. I am glad. She will have to stay with us for a few days, as Mrs. Poppen wanted to paint the room before the next boarder moved in.

At supper, Aunt Julia was quiet; she looks at Janice as if she had crawled out from under a rock. When Janice had gone to the bathroom and didn't help with dishes, Aunt Julia whispered about her make-up and nail polish.

The vicar stopped by after supper to talk to Dad. Janice flirted so much with the two of them that she had them both blushing. I smiled through it all, even though it made me feel funny.

Friday, September 5, 1947

I spent the day organizing my classroom and putting up a bulletin board. Everything is ready. The room had been painted over the summer; it looks so fresh and clean. I unpacked all the new reading books. I am really excited about the new *Alice and Jerry books.* I am really looking forward to this year.

I have decided that after the Pledge and Lord's Prayer we will sing two songs this year, one a patriotic or folk song and the other a hymn. The young people are just not learning the old hymns.

Saturday, September 6, 1947

I tried to talk to Mrs. Speck again. She was not at the hotel, and when I went to the house, Betty whispered through the screen door that she was sleeping and not to be bothered. She had stayed up late working at the hotel. Betty says her mother gives back rubs to help people sleep. I am glad the girls have not figured out what their mother is really doing. Gracious, what an example she is to her girls!

In the afternoon, when I went back to the hotel, Mrs. Speck was there. Our conversation was almost as pleasant as the previous one.

Me: Hello, Mrs. Speck, how are you?

Her: Yeah.

Me: I stopped in earlier, and the girls said you were sleeping.

Her: I work.

Me: Yes, I imagine it must be hard providing for those girls all by yourself.

Her: Did you hear me complain?

Me: When Mr. Anderson was here, my aunt purchased some fabric and sewed a few dresses for the girls. She also bought them some used shoes.

Her: Then why ain't *she* talking to me?

Me: She did it for me while I was in Aberdeen.

Her: Yeah, I heard you were off playing school.

Me: I was taking classes.

Her: I am sure you need all the help you can get.

Me: We have all these dresses that were made and shoes for the girls. I was wondering if we could give them to them.

Her: It's a free country ain't it? I don't care what you do. Just don't give them no shoelaces. They ain't 'loud to have laces.

Me: May I ask why?

Her: I'm their mom, and I say so. Rose ate one once and pooped and barfed string for a week. I cain't have that happen again. If you ever get any kids, you will understand. But you probably won't ever find a man. You gotta know how to treat a man to get one.

Me: We found slip on loafers for Betty, but only tie shoes for the little girls.

Her: You gotta hearing problem? I-said-no-shoelaces.

Me: Well, we will look into something different for the girls. Would it be all right if I give the dresses to them today, so they can have them for Monday?

Her: I don't care what you do with your time. Me, I'm busy. I work for a living. I don't have time to stick my uppity nose in other people's business. If you worked instead of sitting around playing school all day, you might understand.

Me: Well, thank you, Mrs. Speck. I will give the clothes to the girls when they stop in this afternoon. You have a good evening.

Her: You too. (And this she said with such sweet sarcasm.)

At lunch, I told Dad about the no shoelaces rule, and he opened his wallet and said go buy them some of the little girl's shoes with buckles. Luckily, Mr. Adus had three pair of matching black Mary Janes. And in the right sizes!

Right after *Terry and the Pirates,* I gave them their dresses and shoes. I wish I were a poet or could write, I would describe their eyes and smiles and sheer delight. Over and over, they told me how they were going to keep them nice and only wear them to school. Betty said she thought people would mistake them for princesses in such beautiful dresses. She wondered if Elizabeth and Margaret had such elegant dresses when they were younger.

The fabric was all dark and serviceable. After the girls' reaction, I wished I were giving them something girly and frilly.

Aunt Doris called after supper to tell me they had stopped to thank her and had each hugged her twice. Next week, I want to take them to Mrs. Gehm's.

The other day, when I showed Aunt Julia my *Neighbor Lady Cookbook,* she grabbed it up. Tonight, she made Potato Turtles from it. It was just a hot dog stuck through a potato and baked; however, it was a pretty good supper. We also had corn on the cob and fresh tomatoes.

There has been no more discussion of Uncle Edvard's things. But Aunt Julia did bring home a few things from the farm, including the white enamelware coffee pot that belonged to *Bestemor.*

I love that old pot. It reminds me of the tea parties of milky coffee and *pepperkake* with Grandmother. When I washed it for her, we talked of those thin crisp gingersnaps and wondered if anyone had her recipe. It was good to have something neutral and cozy to speak about with Aunt Julia. She said that it was one of the first things they bought when they came to the U.S. That made it even harder for me to give it up. However, if it calms Aunt Julia down, I can part with it. She also took the quilt off the bed that the vicar was using and some of Uncle Edvard's sweaters for Uncle Al.

I wish I could be more generous of heart. I would like to think of all that Aunt Julia did for me, just so I could go to college. All I can think of is her sharp tongue and how she can wound Dad with only a look or word.

Sunday, September 7, 1947

I had not realized it, but since Aunt Julia has been here, Dad had gone back to St. Paul's. That is where we went today.

It was so hot today, but Aunt Julia made use of my cookbook again, and made Oven Meat Croquettes, with corn, beets, cucumbers, and tomatoes from the garden. The kitchen was hot, so I laid the table in the dining room.

She invited Mrs. B. and the vicar to join us. He got quite excited when he talked about the ball team and his job. He likes that he has met so many people through those situations. He said that he hopes to have enough money saved to have his mother join him later this autumn.

As she served the coffee, Aunt Julia got to talking about rationing during the war and how nice it was to drink all the coffee she wanted and not have to reuse the grounds or add anything to it. Her friends had used dried dandelion roots to make coffee go further. She likened rationing to starvation.

The vicar's face turned somber and dark. He quietly said that the rationing we had here in the US did not compare to the starvation he saw in Europe.

Again, Aunt Julia continued talking and talking about rationing and how she could only make a cake once a month because of the lack of sugar. "Can you imagine? Only one cake a month?"

The vicar tried to explain that rationing was not the same as starvation. Aunt Julia just rattled on. Finally, Dad told her that she *samtaler tull som en gammel høne.* That shut her up for a bit.

The vicar looked at me with raised eyebrows. Later, I whispered *samtaler tull som en gammel høne—*she talks nonsense like a silly old hen.

I am thinking of giving her the cookbook as a thank you for all she did for us. I believe she will use it more than I.

After dinner, the vicar and I took a walk and went past the new church. They started on it while I was gone. It is quite large. The sign out front declares it as the NEW AMERICAN LUTHERAN CHURCH.

The vicar needed to order some clothes and asked to borrow our Montgomery Ward's catalog.

As he left, Aunt Julia told him, "Be sure to return that catalog, young man; they are not free, you know."

Dad turned and said, "Why Julia, yes they are."

Monday, September 8, 1947

A new year with new students. Is there any better day than the first day of a new school year?

As is tradition, we began the day with an assembly. Mr. Warren welcomed the students and lined out the school rules. Even with his use of first person plural, Mr. Warren is able to keep control of the school. The older students do make fun of him behind his back.

I got a bit teary as he called my name and dismissed the first graders to go to their room.

This year I have twenty-five students. Lily and Rose and Violet are in my room. I seated them together until after first recess; they spent a lot of time chattering, so I separated them to the far corners of the room. This, I quickly figured out, was not the answer. Instead of whispering, they shouted across the room to each other. So, I moved them back together. Rose is the dark one, Lily and Violet look so much alike I wonder if they are not twins. I will figure out a way to tell them apart.

* * * * *

Andrew O'Brien
1900 Frank Str.
Aberdeen, South Dakota
September 8, 1947

Dear Hanna,

Thank you for your letter. It was waiting for me when I got home. I was pleased to receive it.

I enjoyed hearing about your life and the girls. Those little girls must keep a lot of you busy.

You said you enjoy reading in the evenings. What are you reading? Would you like to read a book together and discuss it through the mail?

Yes, I did go to Mount Rushmore. It is really an inspiring sight. I had always thought it silly or strange to carve a mountain, but I think differently now. It inspires one to greater patriotism.

I was surprised my car made it. I arrived on Tuesday evening and camped and did quite a bit of hiking until Friday. On Friday, I drove part of the way home and spent the night by the side of the road. Then I drove the rest of the way on Saturday. It would have been nice to have someone with me. Do you enjoy camping and hiking?

I am ready for school to start tomorrow. I will be teaching six classes. Botany, Earth Science, Zoology, Biology I, Biology II, and Advanced Biology.

Mrs. Baum has found two new boarders to take Janice's and your place. Well, no one could ever replace you. But two new young women have moved in, both work at jobs downtown. They are sisters named Marlene and Carlene. They are as different as night and day.

I think Janice moving to De Smet will add some spice to your life. I hope it does not get too spicy and you forget me.

I hope your week goes well. I continue to look forward to hearing from you.

Sincerely,
Andrew O'Brien

* * * * *

Tuesday, September 9, 1947

Aunt Julia went to the De Smet Ladies' Book Club and then told us all about it at supper. Mrs. Roberts served nine different kinds of cookies from the *Your Neighbor Lady Cookbook.* Aunt Julia's favorite was something called Plantation Creams. She asked for my cookbook to copy it. I gave my cookbook as a gift to her. With tears in her eyes, she held it to her breast and said, "Thank you from the bottom of my heart."

She could not remember any of the book discussion; I am sure it was not as important as nine different varieties of cookies.

She did remember that several of the women think the vicar should shave. At this, she turned to Dad and told him that he should also shave; beards were so old fashioned. He smiled and said that he was too old to start shaving.

Wednesday, September 10, 1947

I walked into a quiet house. It took me a minute to understand why. Aunt Julia had left on the 2 P.M. train.

I sat and enjoyed the silence and a cup of tea until Betty and Lily and Rose and Violet showed up to listen to *Terry and the Pirates.*

While they listened, I made a simple supper. I opened a jar of canned chunk pork and fried it; we also had cottage cheese and tomatoes, sliced cucumbers, and beets. I made the beets my favorite way with bacon and a sweet and sour dressing. Dad did not say anything. Tomorrow he will get beets the way he likes them.

On the spare bed were *Bestemor's* coffee pot, the quilt, and the sweaters. Aunt Julia had left a note saying she decided she could not take them. She felt they might be too much of a reminder of how she had treated Uncle Edvard. It surprises me that she feels guilty for the way she treated him.

I feel guilty for being so stingy. It was only an old coffee pot, why was I so glad to have it back? I made a pot of coffee in it for supper.

After tasting it, Dad said, *"Kaffe smaker bedre av denne gamle gryten."* I do not know if it tastes any better in that old pot, but it feels cozy.

Thursday, September 11, 1947

The vicar stopped by after work to talk to Dad. He had gone to the telephone office to make a long distance call during his lunch break to talk to the bishop. He seemed really confused. The secretary that answered the phone did not recall receiving any letters from the vicar but did remember a message last spring about a new priest coming from New York, but he thought the priest called and said that he was not coming after all. The vicar is now talking about another trip to Sioux Falls.

Friday, September 12, 1947

The first week of school is over. I feel good about this year. Lily and Rose and Violet have settled in nicely. They try so hard and are so eager to please.

I walked out to the farm to help with the garden. I fried some chicken and made a thick gravy, boiled fresh potatoes, green beans, and of course, set out as much garden produce as I could put on the table, tomatoes, cucumbers, kohlrabi, and cantaloupe.

The vicar joined us.

As I walked home, I picked a huge bouquet of sunflowers. The ditches are full of them this year.

Saturday, September 13, 1947

Dad and I spent most of the day at the farm in the orchard. Aunt Julia put up a lot of applesauce, and now the storing apples are ripening on the trees. Betty and the girls came out in the morning and spent the day with us. I had not expected them and did not have enough lunch ready. But they filled up on apples.

I also shredded the late cabbage and made sauerkraut. I had enough kraut for both five gallon crocks. I put the girls to work stomping. I am going to leave the stoneware crocks at the farm. The vicar said that although he had learned to like kraut, he knew nothing about making it, but would be glad to watch the crocks. I am pleased to have the smell of sauerkraut at the farm and not in the house.

I had put some beans and Boston brown bread in the oven to slowly bake all day. It was done just on time. There was a chill in the air as we drove home.

When we walked into the house, it smelled of Pinesol and lemon oil. Looking around, we could see someone had cleaned the house while we were at the farm. My guess is Mrs. Callahan did it; it would be just like her.

Sunday, September 14, 1947

I got up early and had three apple pies in the oven before breakfast. The vicar came while we were eating breakfast and joined us. He had breakfast at the farm, but still had room for more. I served one of the pies.

Today we drove out to the St. Petri Church. The Nelsons invited us to dinner. I brought the other two pies along.

Of course, most of the dinner conversation was about the merger and tearing down their church building. The Nelsons are resigned, but very sad. Melvin Wiese had also visited them and told them they were standing in the way of progress. He told them about the new road, and that he was planning on remarrying. Melvin Wiese had picked out "a fairly good one, she was passable and would do." I pity the girl he picks out.

When we got home, Betty and Lily and Rose and Violet were waiting on the porch. We listened to the *Adventures of Terry and the Pirates* and ate the rest of the pie. The vicar stayed and listened with us. Betty snuggled up to me, but the three little girls sat on his lap, which caused a smug look to appear on his face. The vicar went to the farm with Dad when he went to chore.

After supper, I went walking and ended up at the farm. Mr. and Mrs. Watkins had stopped in to visit the vicar, so I joined them on the porch. They then insisted on driving me home.

Monday, September 15, 1947

The other teachers are not happy with Janice. She always forgets to go out for her recess duty. They are afraid to talk to Mr. Warren about it. Neither he nor Janice are shy about talking about their relationship. I was going to talk to her but decided I was not her supervisor, and it was not my problem.

Since two of us are scheduled for each recess, I suggested to the others that we just stop by her room on the way out and remind her.

It is only the third week of school. I do not know why some people must make an issue of everything.

After school, I prepared a crock of End of the Garden Pickles. The sweet vinegary brine for the pickles made the house smell cozy and winter like. Once they are fermented, I will can them.

I fixed pork chops, with apples and onions, and beets with, of course, butter and salt and pepper for Dad.

I was just taking a pie out of the oven when the vicar knocked. He said he smelled it from the depot and hurried over. I gave him a plate of supper; he protested a bit and then ate. He talked about his job and became quite animated as he told some silly stories about Mr. Sweeney. In many ways, the vicar is a different man than he was a few months ago when he came to town, yet he is still haunted by something.

*****

Andrew O'Brien
1900 Frank Str.
Aberdeen, South Dakota
September 15, 1947

Dear Hanna,

It seems as if you had a busy week. I am glad school is going well for you. It sounds as if those triplets are taking up quite a bit of your time. It is too bad their older sister taught them to read. However, that does give you more time for the other students, but I see where it gives them time to make trouble for their beautiful teacher.

I am having a bit of a struggle keeping up with preparing for class lectures and grading. I am enjoying the semester so far, though.

I have a nice group of students. Most are too young to have served in the war. They seem to have a very carefree attitude toward life.

No, I do not attend church. Yes, I do believe. It seems that since the war, I have been very unsettled. While flying and seeing the enemy's planes dive at us, I did a lot of praying. However, since then, I have fallen into an apathetic or unsettled state. I ask myself many questions. I have found no answers.

What brought you joy today?

Sincerely,
Andrew O'Brien

Tuesday, September 16, 1947

Mrs. B. brought Lily and Danny Vincent in each by an ear. It seems that he called her a guttersnipe and she laid into him with both fists and bit him several times. Then Rose and Violet joined in. Betty tried to separate them all and got hit in the eye. She is going to have quite a shiner. Lily's dress got torn.

While trying to separate them Mrs. B.'s hair got pulled. Someone actually pulled out a chunk of hair. She parted her hair to show me her scalp, and it is black! She has died her hair so long that she has turned the scalp black. I found that far more surprising and unusual than a silly schoolyard scrap.

After their radio program, the girls and I talked about words not having meaning and that we can always choose to be kind.

Lily listened very thoughtfully and said, "Well I am going to be kind and tell that Danny he is stinky like chicken guts and see how he likes it."

Wednesday, September 17, 1947

Today I was able to tell the difference between blonde Lily and Violet. Lily walked into school proudly sporting a black eye. The children all gathered around her and admired it.

Betty also walked in this morning with a shiner; however, she hung her head in shame.

Throughout the morning, Danny and Lily would look at each other and make faces or shake their fists. Morning recess went without a fight, but they must have been making war plans. The room buzzed with whispering. When we prayed before lunch, I quickly added a sentence: "Lord, help us love our enemies."

After lunch, Mrs. B. brought Lily in by her pigtail. She had been throwing rocks at Danny, and, according to Mrs. B, he had done nothing to provoke it.

For story hour, I found a tale in Uncle Arthur's books about Donavon and heaping coals on your enemies' head and had a long talk about how we are all friends and get along in first grade.

The talk and story weren't very effective.

Mr. Warren, who was doing Janice's afternoon recess duty, brought in both Danny and Lily. Danny's shirt sleeve was hanging loose, and he had the beginnings of a black eye. Lily's pocket was torn off her dress, she was crying, and it looked as if he had raked his nails down her arm.

"We must do something about this. We cannot have these two young hoodlums continuing this dastardly behavior. We cannot let them go to recess for the rest of the week. We will monitor them in our room." He dusted off his pants, straightened his jacket, turned on his heel and marched out.

I hugged them both and stopped the tears, then took them to the office where Irene helped me clean them up.

Danny was quite insistent he had not scratched her. "No, ma'am I amn't no girl and fight dirty. I hit her fair and square. She'll learn not to call me piggy boy."

While the students were coloring, I wrote a note to both sets of parents.

Thursday, September 18, 1947

Mr. Vincent brought Danny to school today. He stomped in frowning. At first, I was a bit worried, but Mr. Vincent told me that if Danny fights again, I was to spank him. He then handed me a stout stick. If that did not work, I was to have Irene call, and he would come to school and take care of it right away and spank him at school.

If he got spanked at school, he would then take Danny to the woodshed later. He said several times that I had his full support.

After Mr. Vincent left, I got a chair and put the stick on the top of the book-shelf. When I stepped off the chair, Danny rushed up and hugged me, telling me I was the best teacher in the world.

The children glowered at each other, but I think an unsteady truce has been drawn, at least on Danny's side.

At home, after the radio program, the girls and I talked about the scratches, and suddenly Violet burst out wailing. She had joined in the fight and wanted to scratch Danny but got Lily instead. She also tore the pocket, trying to pull Lily away from the fight.

I asked them how their mother received the note and the black eyes. Rose offered up that their mother showed them how to fight by hitting and then backing away and then running in and kicking.

Betty told me they had practiced this new fighting technique until they knocked over a chair and "I got a whoopin' for not keeping them quiet and not making damn sure that Danny left Lily alone."

Saturday, September 20, 1947

Mrs. Walter was at the post office. It does make me wonder why I often run into her there. Does she live there? Does she spend hours there waiting for me? Haha!

Anyway, she told me she had heard from a reliable source that the vicar was drunk and walked home from the Clock Bar singing loudly with a group of men. I told her that surely, they were mistaken. But she was not to be detoured in her mission to speak badly of others. She wondered aloud if that is why the diocese took the church away from him.

Sunday, September 21, 1947

Today we drove to St. Matthew's church. It is the last church in our area to have divided seating. I sat with the women on one side. I do remember sitting on the woman's side between Mom and Grandmother. I would lean over and be jealous of David with Dad, Uncle Edvard, and *Bestefar.* Grandfather always looked so stern in church.

We took our time getting home and stopped at Lake Thompson for a late picnic lunch of fried chicken, coleslaw, baked beans, and apple pie. The vicar started a fire and boiled water for coffee.

Monday, September 22, 1947

Betty came into my classroom late, sobbing and threw herself on my lap. After a long while, she calmed down enough to talk. Mrs. B. requires her to write with her right hand. Anyone can see that her hand dangles uselessly at her side. When she could not do it, she had to stay after school for being disobedient. I am not sure how to handle this.

Dad said it was none of my business since Betty has a mother who should be aware of what is happening.

I looked at him and through my tears said, "But Daddy."

He just said, "But Hanna."

I countered with, "Aunt Julia would raise a ruckus."

"Yes, she would, but you, thankfully, are not Julia."

* * * * *

Andrew O'Brien
1900 Frank
Aberdeen, So. Dak.
09/22/47

Dear Hanna,

Goodness Miss Morland, it sounds as if you have had quite a week with your boxing club. Have you thought of giving them each a pair of boxing gloves and letting them fight it out?

I must say that when I read your letter, I could not help but laugh as you described the fights. Since the men teachers get extra pay for coaching sports, you should request additional compensation for refereeing boxing matches.

We can only imagine what William Warren will say. "We must not fight us." I am still surprised that Janice set her sights on him. We wonder why.

I have been collecting specimens for my biology classes. It has been so beautiful walking in the country. The sloughs are full of waterfowl as they prepare to fly south. I was able to snare a mink and am working on curing the hide.

One morning I came across a cedar tree with unique coloring. As I got closer, I found it was a large number of Monarch butterflies with their wings folded, resting before they continued south.

The one thing that would have improved my roamings is if you had been at my side.

I have started reading the Book of John at your request. I find it most interesting. I am not sure that I can believe it all. So many scholars consider science to be incompatible with the Bible. Do I need to throw my knowledge of science out the window when I become a Christian?

Have you given it any more thought to reading a book together? Have a great week. Think about me.

> *Most Sincerely,*
> *Andrew O'Brien*

* * * * *

Tuesday, September 23, 1947

I could see Betty sitting in the hall on a chair, banished from Mrs. B.'s classroom. I wondered what she had done this time. I remember myself sitting in the same chair, often banished for being a know-it-all.

Hoping not to be caught, I tiptoed down the hall and told her I was looking forward to listening to *Terry and the Pirates* and their adventures. She did manage a smile.

Wednesday, September 24, 1947

When Betty and Lily and Rose and Violet came to listen to their radio program, Betty looked as if she had been crying again. I turned on the radio in the living room and sat with them on the couch. If Betty had sat any closer, she would have been on my lap. I do not know how to comfort her. She told me she hates school and Mrs. B. picks on her.

It has only been a few weeks, and Mrs. B. has already selected her target.

I told Betty that she needed to find ways to see Mrs. B.'s good qualities. We listed a few…she has a lovely singing voice, her hair is always combed, when she reads aloud it is if the book were alive, and she knows her multiplication tables up to the fives (this caused a fit of giggles).

Oh, how I wanted to tell her that Mrs. B. is one of the most awful people that ever lived.

I had to give her an extra-long hug when she left.

In my fourth grade class, I think Mrs. B. picked on Mike first. He breathed too loudly or something like that. Years later, Mike told me that, at first, he was glad she eventually left him alone, but he felt so awful when I became her target.

I clearly remember the day we were working on our multiplication tables, and I corrected her, 7 x 8 was 56, not 54. I told her that it was easy to remember, my grandpa told me a trick: 5-6-7-8. She turned on me with a gleam in her eye. "Oh, my but are we not a smart one and Grandpa is ever so clever. I wonder if he learned that in Germany. He can barely speak English, but he knows his times tables."

Not realizing that she was being mean, I repeated the clue to her in Norwegian. *"Bestefar sier at syv ganger åtte er femti og seks, du må huske fem, seks, syv, åtte."* That caused me to have to endure a lecture on how to be an American, and not speak "horrid foreign gibberish."

For the rest of the year in her classroom I was called Little-Miss-Know-It-

All. Tim Weise was the only student that joined her taunting. The other children looked horrified and did not know how to help. At recess, The Girls would often gather around me and comfort me. Once they made a circle around me, holding hands, and they chanted "be invisible," hoping that if I were invisible, she could not pick on me.

At church, Mrs. B. would come up and hug me and tell me how much she was looking forward to Monday and school.

Mom and Dad would listen, but they always supported the teacher. I was to look for ways to see good things about Mrs. B.

All these memories and missing Mom welled up as I made supper. Amid my tears, there was a knock at the back door. It was the vicar.

He asked me if I was all right, reaching out as if he wanted to hug me. I fell into his arms and had a good cry. His strong arms and broad chest were very comforting.

I told him I had been cutting onions. "Those must have been some onions," was all he said.

Dad walked in as this was going on, only to cause me to start crying all over again and cling to him. I am not sure if I was crying from embarrassment this time or from the memories.

I quickly finished making supper, bacon and tomato sandwiches, a cucumber salad, and kohlrabi with cheese sauce. It could freeze any day, and we won't have this good produce.

After the vicar was gone, Dad asked me what that had been about. I told him about fourth grade and what had happened. It all spilled out. He sat there with tears welling up in his eyes. He said he was so sorry and that they probably should have talked to Mrs. B., but they wanted to support the teacher.

Thursday, September 25, 1947

I woke up feeling as if a weight had been lifted from my heart. Dad met me with a hug. Everything is right in my world again.

School went smoothly. Except at lunch, Mrs. B. came up to me and said Betty had not done or turned in an assignment for two weeks. She will get all Fs on her report card. I asked her if she could complete them in the evenings.

She said, "Absolutely not! All my assignments must be completed during the day where I can monitor the cheaters!"

Walking home, the sky was filled with the clamor of migrating geese.

The field peas are dried, so Dad started thrashing them. He said that this was the last year he was going to raise field peas. He does not think anyone else still raises them, there is no market, and he cannot get parts for the stationary thrasher any longer.

I am not sure what he is going to do with the peas since there is no market. We may eat a lot of dried pea soup this winter.

He has only the corn left to harvest.

Friday, September 26, 1947

I decided that if I would just talk to Mrs. B. as an adult and suggest she allow Betty to write with her left hand that maybe this whole thing could be solved.

I did not ask Dad his opinion; I knew what he would say.

I went in early to ask Irene what she thought. She has been the school secretary for at least the last fifteen years and knows everything that goes on at school. As a ruse, I asked her to help me get some paper in the supply closet. Then shut the door and whispered to her what was going on with Betty.

She said she wonders every year who will be Mrs. B.'s next victim. She has seen Betty in the hall crying and wondered what was happening. She warned me to stay out of it. My talking to Mrs. B. would only make matters worse.

I asked why nothing had been done all these years. Irene said that for the most part people have felt sorry for Mrs. B. since her husband left her and she had to work to make a living and pay back his debts. When he came back and then died within weeks, that only made matters worse. No one wanted to talk to her. It was always the children's word against hers, and people think a teacher would not lie.

She gave me a hug and said she would see what she could do behind the scenes.

What a day! Lily and Danny have avoided each other all week. There had been no name calling or fights. Until afternoon recess! I was on duty and turning the jump rope for some of the girls when suddenly on the other side of the playground there was a huge clamor. Lily was spread out on the ground with children holding her down. A line of children surrounded Danny with his older brother and Emmitt standing on either side of him.

All the stories, except Lily's, are the same. Lily started calling Danny names. He walked away and she continued to follow him yelling and throwing gravel at him. The other children did not want Danny to get a spanking, so they stepped in. It took eight children to keep her down, two on each arm and two on each leg.

Lily said she was doing nothing, just walking around and suddenly, a group of children jumped on her. My initial thought was, "That *is* a common occurrence." I was able to hold my tongue instead and say, "Lily it is important that you tell the truth."

Saturday, September 27, 1947

I needed a day by myself, so I took the pickup and drove to Lake Henry and Lake Thompson. I walked around, sat and read, and ate a picnic lunch. How I enjoyed the quiet.

Sunday, September 28, 1947

We went to St. Petri's for church and were invited to the Nelson's for dinner. After the dishes were done Lydia and I went for a walk. She lost another baby last month. I wish I were as wise as *Bestemor* or Mom and knew what to say. I could only cry with her and offer to pray. They have decided to take in some children from the Children's Home Society.

Monday, September 29, 1947

Betty was wearing her dunce cap again today and spent most of the day in the hall. Mrs. B. would not let her go to the restroom, and she wet herself. She sat there in her humiliation.

** * * * **

Andrew O'Brien
1900 Frank St.
Aberdeen, South Dakota

Dear Hanna,
    It is Sunday afternoon, and I am in my room.
    The kitchen girls have been busy baking, so I have some cookies with my coffee.
    How was your week?
    Your three students and all their troubles sound overwhelming. I

am surprised the mother is so unconcerned. Maybe that is the way of the world; parents are just too busy to care for their children.

That is one biblical proverb I can subscribe to though… Train up a child in the way he should go.

You asked about my family. Dad and Mom still farm down near Vermillion. That is why I went to Dakota State, it was close to home. I have four brothers, and they are all married and having families. I would really like to join them in that. Do you know anyone who would be interested in marrying me?

I really wonder how you do it with teaching, caring for the house, and helping your dad on the farm. I am glad you still have time to write to me.

Last evening, we all walked to the band shell. It was the final concert of the year. There was a bonfire, and the city served potatoes baked in the fire.

I had quite a few unit tests this past week, and I am behind in my grading.

I hope your week is peaceful.
Andrew O'Brien

* * * * *

Tuesday, September 30, 1947

Betty was again in the hall. I saw Irene sneak her a hug. I am not surprised at how Betty has won the hearts of all the other teachers. Behind her clear eyes there is a gentle heart.

After school, I decided I did not want to go home, but needed a walk. I walked south along the slough. The sounds of the geese and ducks coming and settling down for the night drove all the noise from my mind and calmed me. I sat for a long time on the bridge, dangling my feet in the cool water, as I watched it flow past. My heart was much calmer as I walked home.

I walked into the house, and there was a note from Dad saying that the vicar had called and wondered if he could come for supper!!! I had not planned supper yet and was hoping to get by with something easy. Like bread and butter!

Any calmness I did have was gone.

I called Myers Butcher Shop, and they did have a small roast. Bob said he would drop it off on his way home.

I sliced it thinly and fried it. I was able to make thick, brown gravy, boiled potatoes, a jar of beans, apple slices and bread and butter.

The vicar arrived with a bouquet of dried grasses and flowers that he picked in the ditches.

He helped with the dishes and talked of Mr. Sweeney and how things were going at the depot. His greatest concern is that Mr. Sweeney has started drinking again and that Mrs. Sweeney has asked him to fetch her husband home from the bar a few times. Mr. Sweeney then sleeps the next day in the little room next to the office.

The vicar started chuckling and then laughed aloud as he told us he had gone to fetch Mr. Sweeney the other day and he would not leave with him unless he promised to sing all the way home. So, the vicar and Mr. Sweeney walked from the bar to his house, singing "Don't Sit Under the Apple Tree."

Dad sat drinking his tea withdrawn inside of himself. Finally, as if waking from sleep, he slowly told us that Mr. Sweeney has battled this demon since the Great War. He has struggled since he came home from France. Dad did not know that Mr. Sweeney had started drinking again. He said he would visit him soon.

Wednesday, October 1, 1947

At breakfast, Dad said he was going to try and talk to Mr. Sweeney today. However, at supper time, he had not done it. Mr. Sweeney had slept in the back room all day. That means the vicar must do the station master's job *and* his own job. He has learned to issue tickets, send, and receive both mail and freight, plus keep the depot clean.

Friday, October 3, 1947

Betty was in the hall again today, with her dunce cap.

I stayed late to grade papers; I was about done when I heard the clicking of Janice's heels in the hallway. I thought she was coming to walk home with me.

She did not come to my room.

Quite soon, I heard the most awful row between Janice and Mrs. B.! Janice was telling her that that poor little girl was never going to write with her right hand and Mrs. B. needed to quit hounding her. Janice could hear Mrs. B. yelling at Betty through the walls and, today in particular, Mrs. B. had made three of Janice's little girls burst into tears.

Mrs. B. started roaring at her and called her names a polite person should never use, much less hear. The next thing I knew Janice was screaming for help.

Mrs. B. had grabbed Janice by the hair and was yanking her back and forth. I ran and pleaded with Mrs. B. to leave her alone, but she would not listen. She was going to "teach that young trollop a lesson." I took hold of Mrs. B.'s arm, and she then started swinging her free hand at me. It was only after Irene and two other teachers showed up that she let go. Janice was holding her head and crying.

Mrs. B. smoothed her dress and said, "I believe it is time everyone went home." She was very dignified as she put on her hat and coat and gloves and tipped tapped away.

We just stood there speechless.

Janice came for supper and spent the night.

Saturday, October 4, 1947

A very quiet Saturday after yesterday.

Janice mostly lay around with an ice pack on her head. "Willie" came to visit her and took her hand and patted it and kept calling her "our dear."

I wondered what Aunt Julia would have to say about Janice lying on the couch all day and often asking for ice or a glass of cool, fresh water.

I did laundry and cleaned the house.

When Betty and Lily and Rose and Violet came for their program, we sat in the kitchen. I told Betty of my plan to help her learn. She was quite pleased with that. I loaned Dad's old schoolbooks and a notebook to Betty. I gave her some assignments, and we will work through the books. She is so bright and soaks up knowledge like a sponge. I really do not understand Mrs. B.; how does she expect Betty to learn anything in the hallway?

Afterward, they all helped cut and roll rag strips for Peggy.

The girls cut the strips so crookedly; Peggy would never be able to use them. I decided to teach them to crochet. Betty caught on quickly. She wound the rags around her right hand and used her left to hook. It was not long before she had many feet of single chain. Betty worked carefully, assuring each stitch was even. I showed her how to wind it back and make the oval for a rug. She looked at me with a huge smile and said, "I can do this!"

The vicar came for supper, and they all rushed to him. He knelt and gave each a hug—but an extra-long one for Betty. He whispered that he has been praying for her.

He brought in a handful of rosehips and asked me what they were. Dad saw them, and his face lit up. He promised to pay the vicar a nickel for each lard pail full he picked.

"No fair!" I declared." You used to pay us only two cents."

The girls then got excited about picking them. The vicar promised to take them next week, and I promised to make *nypesuppe* if they got enough rosehips.

Dad greedily said that he may not be willing to share the soup if I made it.

I tried calling Mrs. Speck to see if the girls could stay for supper, but there was no answer, and she was not at the hotel. They stayed for supper, and the vicar walked them home.

I baked some sausage and made biscuits, with *fruktssuppe.* There was one ripe tomato yet, so I sliced that. I had planned to secretly enjoy the tomato by myself but decided I shouldn't be so greedy.

Monday, October 6, 1947

After school, Mr. Warren talked to Mrs. B. about her treatment of Janice and Betty. You could not hear what he was saying, but her roaring echoed through the building. I did not want to hear, so I slipped out.

* * * * *

Andrew O'Brien
1900 Frank Str.
Aberdeen, South Dakota
Oct. 6, 1947

Dear Hanna,

I trust you had a pleasant week.

I always rush home on Fridays, knowing that you had written on Wednesday and your letter would be in the mail. There was no letter waiting for me. I knew it would be there on Saturday. It was not. I even looked under the hall table, thinking it fell under it. You must have had a busy week; otherwise, I am sure you would have written. I imagine you are busy with those little girls.

It warms my heart how you have taken to them. Those girls do not have much of a family, but you are providing one.

I bought a bicycle so that I can go even further on my roamings. After a day of teaching and being inside it feels good to cruise the roads looking for new specimens.

I like your idea of reading Les Miserables. *I read it in college but could not make heads or tails of it. This time it is much more enjoyable. How do you want to discuss it through letters? Should we just have a discussion of each chapter?*

I have an idea! You come up on the train every Saturday, and we will discuss the book over supper.

I hope to hear from you soon.

> *Most Sincerely,*
> *Andrew O'Brien*

* * * * *

Tuesday, October 7, 1947

Janice came to see me and was quite pleased with her "Willie." She said he told Mrs. B. that she could not treat children or other teachers that way. She says that she aches all over, and it is as if the hair pulling pulled everything in her.

Wednesday, October 8, 1947

The county superintendent and the school board came to visit. Mr. Brock and Mr. Dawley spent just a few minutes in my room.

At lunch, Mrs. B. came to tell me that they had spent most of the morning in her room. She said she was able to demonstrate for them what a well-run classroom looked like. She did not have to go to college to learn to teach. It just came naturally for her.

Oh Lord, why do you give me so many opportunities to be kind?

I told her I was sure they had a pleasant visit.

Betty told me later that although Mrs. B.'s words are kinder, her face and eyes are not.

Thursday, October 9, 1947

We had our first killing frost. Our long summer has ended.

A quiet day at school.

It was cold and misty all day. The corn is dry enough that Dad has started picking it.

A locomotive exploded at the Lake Preston depot last night. The night watchman was killed. He was new in town.

Friday, October 10, 1947

The vicar called and asked if I would alter some shirts he had ordered from a catalog. They were too big and needed to be taken up. I invited him to eat supper with us.

School moved at a snail's pace. I do not know what made me so antsy today.

I stopped at Peschl's and got some nice looking pork chops. I baked them in the Dutch oven with apples and onions, opened a jar of beans, and fried some potatoes. I could not decide whether to bake a pie or a cake but decided to stir up a hot milk cake with Lazy Daisy Icing.

After supper, the vicar tried on his shirts and showed me how the shoulder seams hung down his arm about three inches. I got flustered while I was pinning the shirt and stuck myself and bled on his new shirt. With the vicar standing there in his undershirt, I became more flustered.

I hope he did not notice.

Saturday, October 11, 1947

I sewed on the vicar's shirts this morning and called and invited him to supper. He said he was going to Mike and Marilyn's house. That bothered me. I called Marilyn to chat and fished for an invitation but did not get one. I was bothered even more. I was bothered that it bothered me and bothered that I did not know why it bothered me. I was bothered all around.

He did stop by afterward and picked up his shirts. I convinced him to stay for a cup of coffee and a piece of sweet potato pie.

Sunday, October 12, 1947

Late in the afternoon, as Dad, the vicar, and I were enjoying a cup of tea on the back porch, Mrs. B. came calling. She asked to talk to Dad alone. He said that what she would have to say to him, she could say in front of us.

She went on to tell "her side of the story." She was only doing her best and trying to teach Betty, but Betty was "incorrigible and refused to obey." In her story, Betty was a tyrant and she the meek, kind teacher.

Dad told her that of all people, who has experienced a lot in life, she should be able to be patient and gentle to a person less fortunate than herself.

He had such a kind way of telling her that she really needed to change. He went on to say that he was sure she understood that Betty should be allowed to use her left hand to write.

He grimaced as she said, "Oh my dear Ernst, you are so right. I shall open my heart to that dear child."

* * * * *

Andrew O'Brien
1900 Frank St.
Aberdeen, South Dakota
October 12, 1947

Dear Hanna,

It was a busy week at school for me, too. It was homecoming and so the week was full of foolishness, fun, and activities. The students could think of nothing other than homecoming. It was a fight to get them to concentrate on their studies. On Tuesday, I decided I should just give in and enjoy it also. So, I did. Except for the dance last night.

I was scheduled to chaperone the dance. I mostly stood off to the side with the other professors and talked about how we wished we were elsewhere.

I got up early this morning and rode my bike in search of specimens. I was going past a small country church as the bell was calling people to worship so I decided to join them. It was a different experience for me. The people were friendly and invited me to join them again. I kept thinking how happy it would make you.

The weather has been pleasant, and I have been able to continue my search for more specimens. Mrs. Baum and her girls have complained about cleaning my room; I have moved a number of the specimens to my office.

I am glad those little girls have settled down into a routine and that your life is a bit easier. I am sorry to report that with all the activities I have not read any this week.

I hope you have a good week. I look forward to hearing from you.

Sincerely,
Andrew

* * * * *

Tuesday, October 14, 1947

The De Smet Ladies' Book Club met today. After school, I walked by Mrs. Danley's house and a few of the women were still there. I was invited in for some left over cake. Today, they discussed *Cannery Row* by Steinbeck. I really enjoyed that book and was glad to hear a few of their thoughts. I liked the gritty characters, but all the stories within the story were a bit confusing.

Sadly, I was also glad for a bit of gossip. The whole town is talking about Mrs. B., Mrs. Speck, and Betty and Lily and Rose and Violet. Mrs. Danley listed who was on whose side. It seems more are concerned about the welfare of the girls than any other.

I kept the information to myself; Dad would not be pleased to know I had so willingly gossiped. We had fried pork sausage, apple and cabbage salad, and green beans.

Saturday, October 18, 1947

Melvin Wiese came to the house today. I told him right away that Dad was at the farm.

Oh my! Oh my! Oh my! He came to tell me that he thinks I would make a good wife for him. Just thinking about it makes me shake. I will try to relate the conversation as it happened.

"Hanna, I have given it a lot of thought and think we should get married."

"I have never thought that," I squeaked. "What makes you think that?"

"Well, my dear, you are fairly good looking, you attend the right church, you understand farm life, you are a passable cook, and you could possibly supply me with more children. You would do for a wife." Here he grabbed the waist band of his pants and pulled on it and said, "It all still works." I wanted to slap him.

"You will inherit the farm, all our land will be joined together, and you will then be part of a family that is actual homesteaders, not one that had bought a relinquishment."

"Oh, my!"

"And most importantly, I think it is God's will for you."

I sat there for the longest time and did not know what to say. I squeaked out, "Have you spoken to Dad about this?"

"No, but I will stop at the farm and announce our engagement."

Drawing up as much inner strength as I could, I remembered Mother saying we should take every chance to be kind.

Be kind.

Kind. How to be kind?

How to be kind?

How to be kind when I wanted to laugh hysterically and run away.

Kind.

Be kind.

"Mr. Wiese."

"Call me Mel."

"Mr. Wiese, I think there are women that might be glad to take you up on your offer. I am not one of them."

"You are saying no?"

"Yes."

"Yes, you are saying yes?"

"No, I am saying, no."

"You are saying, no?"

"Yes, I am saying no."

"Well, who are you interested in? Certainly not that hairy preacher or that silly prissy pants principal."

"I am not interested in marrying you."

"And why not? I just told you all the reasons why we should get married. I think it is God's will for you. Think of the money you will have."

At this point, the vicar came up the walk and stood there. I was so glad to see him; I almost ran and hugged him. Instead, I took two steps toward him and gave him a look of gratitude.

"I asked you, who you are interested in?"

"Mr. Wiese, that is not important. What is important *is* that I will not marry you. And it is also not for you to say what God's will is for me."

"Who are you interested in?"

"I am not going to marry you or tell you in whom I am interested."

"I asked you, who are you interested in? Remember what the Bible says about women being submissive."

"Mr. Wiese, I am not interested in marrying you."

"You need to answer me. Who are you interested in?"

The vicar answered for me. "Mr. Wiese, I do not think it is a matter of in whom she is interested. She has told you clearly that she is not interested in marrying you. I am sure you understand a woman is called to be submissive to her husband who in turn is submissive to God."

Turning various shades of purple, he stomped off shouting, "You will regret this!"

I walked around the house and sat on the back porch. I wanted to cry. The tears would not come. I felt only anger. What a mockery he made of everything I hold dear!

The vicar made a cup of tea and brought it to me; sitting next to me, he put his arm around me. I leaned on him and had a good cry.

We were sitting there when Dad came and said, "Ahh Hanna, I forgot to tell you, I invited Jacob for supper."

After telling Dad the complete account, he took us to the Ritz Café for supper. His jaw muscles worked in and out even when he was not chewing. I was so glad Janice and "Willie" happened to be there; sitting and listening to them gave us something else to think about.

On the way home, Dad said we should all go to Brookings to church tomorrow.

Sunday, October 19, 1947

The vicar got here early, and we all piled into the pickup. We mostly drove in companionable silence.

I had brought a thermos of coffee, so we stopped at the park in Arlington for a break.

It was a cold, yet comfortable ride being squeezed between Dad and the vicar.

After church, the vicar had a long conversation with the priest. I wish, for his sake, that this problem could be solved. I visited with the wife, Jane; she is such a comfortable person. She is a good listener and has an infectious giggle.

We ate dinner at a diner downtown. I did not think anyone would notice, so I slipped off my shoes. As the vicar adjusted himself in his seat, he touched my feet several times. At first, he blushed and then, the next time, he turned to me and said, with his eyes crinkling, "I think there is an odor of smelly feet in here."

I blushed.

Dad just looked at us and said, "I don't smell anything but fried chicken."

Dad stopped at the Johnson's in Volga. We went in for coffee and a fast paced conversation.

The vicar did not get antsy and seemed quite content to spend the day with us.

I fell asleep on the way home, only to wake and find my head on the vicar's shoulder. To add to my embarrassment, while sleeping I slobbered and made a damp spot on his coat.

Monday, October 20, 1947

With Aunt Julia, Mr. Sweeney and Melvin Wiese on his mind, Dad has withdrawn into himself.

A letter from Andrew arrived. They continue to come weekly. What a quandary!

* * * * *

Jacob Stewart
General Delivery
De Smet, South Dakota
October 20, 1947

Dear Father Paul,

I hope you will forgive the informal greeting, but I am writing as a friend and not as a subordinate.

I would like your advice on several plaguing issues. The first being the parish and the local bishop. I have visited with the local priests several times and they all assure me his reaction and behavior are so unlike him. They and Mr. Morland continue to encourage me to make an appointment and visit with him again. I know this is the best sort of action. I have talked to the station master a few times about taking a few days off and going to Sioux Falls.

I cannot make myself go. There are so many what-ifs. What if he does not see me? What if I am never allowed to serve the congregation? My mind reels with the questions. It is easier to do nothing. I fear facing the future and failing.

Involved with this are my feelings for Miss Morland. She fills my every waking thought. I look into her blue eyes, and my heart races and my hands shake. How I long to hold her and get lost in her eyes. It is difficult for me to decipher how she feels about me.

My nights continue to be plagued with memories and visions of Europe. I feel I should be doing more to ease the suffering caused by the war. Do you think the Lord is telling me to join in the relief efforts? Is that why the door has closed here in De Smet? I believe I have saved enough for my fare to Europe.

Since Dad's death you have in so many ways provided guidance and direction. I need that now. Please pray for me that I would know the Lord's leading and decide.

I remain,
Your servant,
Jacob

* * * * *

Andrew O'Brien
1900 Frank St.
Aberdeen, South Dakota
October 19, 1947

Dear Hanna,

I need to be honest. I spend a lot of time daydreaming about you. I imagine you in a little house near the college campus waiting for me to come home. Fixing supper. Tending our children. Managing the home. Making my life complete.

I have not been able to tell from your letters if you have any feelings for me or if you are really interested in continuing our correspondence.

Andrew

* * * * *

Tuesday, October 21, 1947

I was at the post office when Mr. Melvin Wiese came in to get his mail. He followed me out and when he caught up to me, he shoved an envelope in my face. It was addressed to "Mr. Melvin Wiese, Proprietor of Wiese Land and Cattle."

Then, without permission, he took my hand, and said, "Just one of the many things you will be missing out on."

I could not pull my hand away fast enough, I felt as if it had been burned.

I wanted to make a bit of a statement. I said very quietly but firmly, "Mr. Weise, you are a neighbor, and I need to be polite to you. From now on, our conversations will only be about the weather. Otherwise, I would rather you not speak to me. Do not ever touch me again."

Looking him directly in the eyes as strongly as I could, I said, "Let-me-re-peat-that, -do-not-ever-touch-me-again."

He stood speechless.

I was not kind.

I left quickly.

Wednesday, October 22, 1947
The Vicar's Birthday

Marilyn invited us to their house for supper to celebrate the vicar's birthday. She made a scrumptious supper, but I was distracted. I wanted to talk to her about Mr. Wiese and Andrew, especially after Andrew's last letter.

I had forgotten to buy a present, but Dad picked up some Red Heel socks and a few wrenches for him. Before we left the house, my eye fell on my knitting, and I realized that the *votter* I had just finished would fit him perfectly. He seemed pleased with them. As he carefully scrutinized the snowflake pattern he said, "I might be mistaken for a Norwegian in these mittens."

When the men settled down in the living room to talk, Marilyn and I slipped into the bedroom with our coffee. We sat on the floor with our backs against the bed and covered our laps with blankets. I started getting all teary right away. In between blubbering, I told her about Mr. Wiese coming to the house and the meeting at the post office. Then we talked about Mr. William Jennings Bryan Warren and that he and Janice were announcing their engagement in next week's paper.

She read the last letter from Andrew and started laughing. She laughed, I cried, we hugged, I hit her. That started us laughing again, and we lost control. We would just look at each other and start laughing.

Finally, I asked her why we were laughing.

Here I was: reasonably good looking, a passable cook, possibly could have children, would inherit the farm, attended the right church, and still single.

Taking hold of my hands and looking me in the eye, she told me, "Just forget Melvin Wiese and Mr. Warren. They were not nearly good enough for you. You need to wait and let this thing with Andrew become clear, and maybe, just maybe you are not looking close enough to home."

She would not tell me who was closer to home. I confided that the vicar was always so distant; I did not think he was interested.

I told her about the comment that I overheard Dad make in Aberdeen, about having suitors and not realizing it. That set her off laughing again.

I need a new best friend. One that is kind.

Thursday, October 23, 1947

I ran into that oily shoe salesman at the grocery store today. He makes me feel so creepy.

Friday, October 24, 1947

The vicar called and asked if he could come for supper. I like that he feels free to do that. But it makes me so antsy anymore. I think I must have everything just right for him. I do not like feeling that way.

School went incredibly slow. I could not get away fast enough.

I made meatballs, gravy, potatoes, corn, and a peach pie.

With the canning done by Aunt Julia and me, the shelves in the storeroom had been full. Already there are many empty jars. With the girls and the vicar to feed, I guess we should have canned more. It makes me feel a bit guilty for going to school.

The vicar wanted to tell Dad and me that he thinks he has saved enough to bring his mother out here. He paid Dad off for all the money he had borrowed. He has enough for her fare and for the freight to bring her things out. He also wants Dad to help him find a car.

The vicar wondered about her staying at the farm with him. Would she want to find work? We talked about the distance, winter, walking, no electricity or running water. REA was supposed to put a line in going north. They started that way about five years ago, but they turned west and went to the Wiese farm instead. That makes the line only a mile away. Dad said he would investigate it. I do not think he really wants to electrify the house. He likes knowing the house is the same as when his parents lived there.

Dad suggested we switch houses.

* * * * *

Jacob Stewart
General Delivery
De Smet, South Dakota
October 25, 1947

Dear Mother,

Please find enclosed a cashier's check for your train fare to South Dakota. There should be enough for you to ship any of the furniture and dishes you wish to bring with you.

I do not know where we will live, but for the time being, you will be staying at the Morland farm with me. It will be very different than your life in the city, but I think you will like it. It will remind you of your childhood on the farm in Maine.

I hope you will not think about getting a job. I would like you to feel comfortable just taking care of the house and me. You know what a big job that has been through the years.

Please let me know when you have taken care of everything and will arrive. I am looking forward to your arrival. We have been apart for too many years.

I believe you will make one last trip to the cemetery to visit Dad. I know you also miss him very much. There are few days that I do not wish he were here. He would love the open prairie and the people here. I think he would very much approve of Miss Morland. I can imagine him teasing her until she blushes bright red. I would like to be able to tease her. But I find her far too intimidating.

Now if only I could think of a way to convince Hanna Morland to approve of me.

I remain,
Your loving son,
Jacob

Sunday, October 26, 1947

It rained all day.

I am glad most of the corn harvest is done and Dad has the farm ready for winter.

Monday, October 27, 1947

It rained all day.

Tuesday, October 28, 1947

It rained all day.

Wednesday, October 29, 1947

The Speck girls have not been in school yet this week, and they did not come for their radio program. I went past their house on the way home. I think they were in there but did not answer the door. I tried phoning several times, and there was no answer.

Thursday, October 30, 1947

I stopped by the De Smet Hotel, and Mr. Spurgeon said Mrs. Speck had quit and told him she was planning to leave town. He thinks she left town with the shoe salesman.

I went to the house again. It seems as if the girls are in there and not answering the door. There was a scraping sound and possibly some whispering.

Friday, October 31, 1947
Halloween

At noon, Mrs. B. came and told me her classroom was quieter and that it smelled better. Good riddance to bad rubbish.

I am not sure what my reply was. I felt as if I had just slowly slumped and disappeared into the floor.

I did imagine myself grabbing her hair and yanking her back and forth as she did Janice.

The children were so excited today. I wish that Lily and Rose and Violet were here to enjoy the fun. After lunch, the children each made a paper bag mask and then we tried to guess who was behind the mask. I brought them some popcorn balls.

They all promised to come to my house trick or treating. They made good on their promises.

Saturday, November 1, 1947

I walked to the girls' house several times. No one answered the door.

The vicar said he thought he saw Betty lurking around the corner of the depot. At dinner time he could not find his lunch pail and wondered if he had left it at home. He went to the Ritz Cafe for lunch and later discovered his empty lunch pail sitting on the dock. All he can figure is that he left it there and did not pack a lunch or Betty took it.

Sunday, November 2, 1947

It was a cold nippy morning. The cold seemed to creep into my bones.

I made monkey bread for breakfast. We drove to North Preston Lutheran Church. I find our church shopping a bit embarrassing, but I am also enjoying all the different sermons and seeing so many people that we rarely see.

Mrs. Axel Larsen was in church. I cannot remember when I saw her last. She is the same with blue hair and bright red lipstick. She grabbed my elbow and steered me off to the side and peppered me with questions and filled me with gossip. She asked me when the vicar was going to propose. I told her we were not even dating; we were just friends.

She had seen Mrs. B. lately and heard from her that Dad had proposed. Emphatically, I told her that was not true.

Somehow, she also knew all about Mr. Wiese and his proposal. My head hurt when she let me go.

When we got home, the rest of the monkey bread was gone as well as the pan of rolls I had made. Did Mrs. Speck go off and leave them at home alone with no food, so they are stealing?

Monday, November 3, 1947

Well, the plot thickens. I feel a bit like Nancy Drew. Perhaps, if teaching does not work out, I could open a detective agency.

I dropped a basket of food off at the depot and the vicar left it on the dock and watched from around the corner. Sure enough, Betty came and took it, and returned it empty later.

When I told the vicar that I felt like Nancy, he said, "Well, just call me Joe."

Dad said he would talk to the sheriff tomorrow.

Tuesday, November 4, 1947

What a day! The sheriff came to the school as I was leaving. He found Betty and Lily and Rose and Violet in the house alone. He was laughing so hard it was difficult for him to tell me. He went to the house and knocked on the door. They came out with their hands up begging him not to shoot.

They said their mother told them they should not leave the house until she returned. They did not know where she went, but she had met a man at the hotel. Lily was adamant that their mother would be back soon.

He asked me if they could stay with me for a few hours.

Together we went back to their house, and I gathered up clothes and such. At my home, I had them take baths. I went in and scrubbed their hair and made sure they were clean. I fed them supper and waited. Those few hours stretched until 9 o'clock.

I had offered that they could stay with us, but he said the law required him to take them to the poor farm. I hated to send them there, but I had to.

Wednesday, November 5, 1947

I used to wish something would happen to make my life more exciting. Not anymore! The sheriff stopped at school around noon to tell me the girls were missing from the poor farm school. No one saw them leave, and they took all their belongings. He wondered if I had seen them.

When I got home, I looked all over and could not find them or any evidence that they had been there.

Before supper, Dad and I drove up and down the roads around the poor farm looking for them.

Thursday, November 6, 1947

Four little chicks were found staying in our barn. The vicar was eating supper and Lily came in and asked for something to eat. He brought them to town. I hugged them and fed them. I cried after the sheriff came and took them back to the poor farm.

Friday, November 7, 1947

I called the poor farm and talked to Betty after school. She said the county school by the farm was ok and that Lily got in a fight with one of the Johnson boys. The teacher and students at the country school do not accept the children from the farm. I promised to come to see them tomorrow.

Saturday, November 8, 1947

I was barely out of bed when the sheriff called to tell us that they had left the poor farm again. This time the sparrows flew as far as our garage. It is incredible they can walk seven miles during the night. When Dad went out to take the pickup to chore, they were sleeping in the back of it.

I fixed them breakfast, and in a short time they were asleep in the living room.

The sheriff stopped in and said he was too busy to take them to the poor farm. Winking at me, he said he would take them when he had time. I think it will be a while before he has time.

So, we spent the afternoon doing laundry and baking cookies. We walked to their house and picked up more of their things. After *Terry and the Pirates,* Betty was content to sit and crochet.

My heart aches for them.

I made cabbage rolls, baked potatoes, baked beans, and applesauce.

The vicar came for supper and was loud and silly with them, chasing and tickling Lily and Rose and Violet. They screamed and giggled.

While Dad read the *Saturday Evening Post,* Betty snuggled up to him and crocheted; they ignored and enjoyed the commotion. She often looked up and would sigh with contentment.

The girls are used to sleeping in one bed, so I put them up in the small room.

Sunday, November 9, 1947

Dad and I had a long discussion about whether the girls should go to church or not. The conclusion was that it was time they learned what church was all about.

So, between combing hair and tying ribbons and straightening dresses they received instructions repeatedly about how to behave in church. Lily was reminded several times that she should not hit or fight with anyone. Rose and Violet promised to keep her in line.

I was amazed when Dad said we would go to St. Paul's. Of course, we got a lot of stares and odd looks…Dad and I with Betty and three ducklings following us and the vicar in his worn-out suit bringing up the rear guard. I am not sure if they stared at our parade or because it has been so long since we had been in church.

Melvin Wiese did not speak to me. But he did corner Dad and talked to him about making a pledge for the new building. He reminded Dad that we had a good wheat crop two years in a row, and we owe it to the church to give abundantly. I heard him loudly say, "Why are you so stingy? I am giving until it hurts."

I do not wholly understand Dad's thoughts and feelings. I know he would not be against a new building if ours were falling apart or overflowing and crowded. He does not mind that the Synod dropped Norwegian from their name; but why does he not like that they call themselves the American Lutheran Church? I wonder if it is tied up in his feelings for Melvin Wiese.

I wish I could say the day went uneventfully. It did not. Lily and Rose and Violet needed endless entertainment.

Mrs. B. just "happened by" and stopped in. Her rudest remark was something about how the house smelled like trash. She went on to tell me I was not wise to let go of Mr. Warren.

When the noise got above a dull roar, Dad suggested we return them to the poor farm. Lily and Rose and Violet instantly panicked.

Betty whispered to me, "Your old dad is kidding. I can tell; his eyes are smiling."

* * * * *

Andrew O'Brien
1900 Frank Str.
Aberdeen, So. Dakota
November 10, 1947

Dear Hanna,

I have not told you, but I have been attending church with the Baums. Your Lutheran services are not too unlike the Catholic services I grew up with. Although I can tell there is a difference in doctrine. The minister loaned me Luther's Small Catechism. *It is interesting reading.*

I have been reading Dickins' Tale of Two Cities *after my school-work is done. I am not very far. And of course, our weekly chapter of* Les Miserables.

Do you really think that woman would go off and leave those girls alone in the house? I am not much of a prayer, but I have prayed they would find a safe and secure home. It has made me even more thankful for my family.

The students are restless and looking forward to Christmas break. Me too!

Sincerely,
Andrew O'Brien

* * * * *

Winter

Tuesday, November 11, 1947

We woke to a frigid house. I had the girls come down and dress by the stove. Once Dad got the furnace going the house warmed up quickly. I made oatmeal with raisins and dates for breakfast. Lily loudly announced that she does not eat oatmeal and wanted two fried eggs. Dad calmly told her that she would learn to eat oatmeal or be hungry until lunch. Rose held Lily's nose, and Violet spooned the "awful stuff" in. All the while, Dad and I sat, coughed, and turned red trying not to laugh. Lily ate her oatmeal. Both of us gave her a big hug, which she received rather stiffly. Trying to hug a fence post would have been easier.

After school, I took inventory of the girls' winter clothes. I cannot believe I did not think of it before today. A few quick calls to Marilyn, Aunt Doris, and a few of The Girls and I had people dropping off all sorts of winter wear at the house. They will be warm and ready. They were even given ice skates. So yes, we are prepared for winter.

I wonder how the discussion went at the De Smet Ladies' Book Club meeting today.

I had put a pan of Boston Baked Beans in the stove before we left for school, and they were perfectly done in time for supper.

I also started a system: one girl helps me make supper, and everyone helps with dishes. It was Betty's turn to cook. She opened the jars of peaches and poured them in a bowl, sliced the rye bread, and set the table. I made a pan of Poor Man's Steak.

Lily and Rose and Violet listened to *Terry and the Pirates* and gave us warning looks if we made too much noise.

The vicar showed up in time for supper; he, of course, stayed. The five of them did dishes while Dad and I listened to the news and then the *Bohemian Band.* When the *Green Hornet* came on the washing stopped, and everyone listened.

Wednesday, November 12, 1947

It was cold enough that I wore my long wool coat. When I walked into school, Janice said, "You look like a nun in that dark blue coat. You should buy something bright."

The vicar found a nice used black Ford at O'Keeffe's. He seems pleased with it. The seats are a bit worn out, and he asked where to buy canvas or rugs to lay on the seats. He said he will still walk to work.

Thursday, November 13, 1947

Toward evening it began to flurry. I got a postcard from Harold Baum.

Friday, November 14, 1947

It snowed all day with no wind. The snow came straight down and blanketed the landscape, bringing a peaceful feeling with it. The children had a hard time concentrating on their work, as usual. What is it with children and snow?

I wasn't getting any work out of them; all they wanted to do was stare dreamily out the window. We cut out snowflakes and painted snow pictures instead.

It is good being friends with the cook. I sent Rosanna a note and asked for some sweetened condensed milk, vanilla, a few big bowls, and a spoon. I dispatched the boys out to bring us plenty of snow. We made snow ice cream.

I was a bit late getting out for afternoon recess, I have so many buckles to fasten and coats to zip and hoods to tie. Good old Mrs. B. came tip-tapping down the hall. She wanted to remind me that if there is an accident while the children are unsupervised, she could never forgive herself.

I am not sure why I just did not get my coat on and go out. I have not been kind lately. I told Mrs. B., "For your peace of mind, you should probably be outside for recess all the time."

Will I never learn to be kind?

Saturday, November 15, 1947

I do not know when I have seen a snowstorm like this one. The snow came straight down for two days layering everything. The radio said we had seventeen inches.

The girls and I bundled up and walked to the farm. Leaving the girls with Dad to "help" him with the chores, I walked on further north. I enjoyed the silence. My feet were cold, but I did not want to stop. In the distance, I could see someone else out walking. As I got closer, I saw it was the vicar. When we met, I turned and started back to the farm with him. After greeting, neither of us said anything. It was a comfortable feeling as we walked back to the farm.

Once we got back to the farm, he invited us all to lunch. He opened three cans of soup and toasted some bread. He seemed to enjoy having company. Afterward we sat around the stove and drank hot chocolate.

It was very comfortable until Lily turned to the vicar and said, "Preacher, you should marry her."

Betty pinched Lily, and she yelped.

Dad stifled a laugh.

Then there was just uncomfortable silence.

* * * * *

Andrew O'Brien
1900 Frank Str.
Aberdeen, So. Dak
November 16, 1947

Dear Hanna,

How are you this week? I enjoyed your letter and hearing about all the adventures you are having with those girls.

Have you gotten any of this snow? It has made walking to school difficult. I took my car several days, but I must park and walk almost as far as when I walk from the Baum's.

I have started looking for my own home. Mr. Kaufmann is watching for furniture and other household items for me. There are a few cottages near the college, but they have such small yards. Children need room to run. I have also applied for a house in the married professor's housing.

Last week, Mr. Kaufmann heard from the Displaced Person's Committee, they think they have located a cousin of his living in Palestine. He was so emotional when he told me that he could hardly talk. He said it was the result of your father's prayers. I believe you know they have struck up quite a friendship through correspondence.

I hope your next week is blessed with joy. I look forward to hearing from you.

Sincerely,
Andrew O'Brien

* * * * *

Tuesday, November 18, 1947

Mrs. B. came up to me first thing in the morning and told me she would no longer tolerate Betty in her class. Betty should go to the state institution in Redfield, where all the retards go.

Betty is far from retarded. She is a bright child, with some physical deformities.

Wednesday, November 19, 1947

As we walked home from school, I spied Mrs. Speck on the front porch smoking. She must have been there a while. The steps were littered with cigarette butts.

When we got closer, the girls started shouting, "Mama! Mama!" and ran to her.

She flicked her cigarette into the snow and started swinging as they got closer all the while saying, "You brats, I told you to stay in the house. I'll teach you to mind me."

Her eye is black, and she has an old yellow bruise on her face.

Me: Hello, Mrs. Speck, how are you? The girls missed you. You must be cold, why don't you come in and warm up?

Her: Hello yourself, you child thief. I went to the house. They weren't there. I figured they would be here. Why don't you leave other people's kids alone and get some of your own?

Me: The sheriff took them to the poor farm, and they ran away and came here. My dad and I have been caring for them since.

Her: Yeah sure, make up a story.

Me: It is good that you are back. Would you like to come in and have a cup of tea or coffee? You are welcome to stay for supper.

Her: Oh, have a little tea party. How sweet. I have better things to do with my time. I need to go to work. Some people work for a living.

Me: Well, come on in and rest a bit while the girls pack their things.

Her: Oh, now I see it. You went into my house and stole stuff; that is trespassing. I will be talking to the sheriff about that.

Me: Mrs. Speck, the girls needed clothes and things. I couldn't let them wear the same thing for the last two weeks.

Her: You should have left them alone. They were just fine in the house.

Me: They were not "just" fine. The girls had run out of food and were stealing. The sheriff found them and took them to the poor farm.

Her: Don't get smart with me little missy. They were fine. I am their mother, I know. They were only taking from the rich and giving it to the poor. Like Robin Hood. I know more than you think.

"Come on girls, get yer stuff and let's go." She then lit up another cigarette. I decided it was best not to say anything more. She only twists words and makes outrageous statements.

The girls grabbed their stuff and were ready to go in a matter of minutes.

As they walked away, I looked at my hands. They were shaking, as were my heart and stomach.

While making supper, I wondered about Mom. In these situations, she would have been kind, gracious, and refined. I kept thinking that if I had a stick, I would have hit Mrs. Speck. Why does she anger me? Why does she cause my insides to boil?

The vicar stopped by after work. He had seen Mrs. Speck and the children walk past the depot and wanted to be sympathetic. I invited him to stay for supper. I had made more than for just Dad and me than I realized.

He reminded me that God was very interested in those little girls, and I could still have a lot of influence over them at school. Before he left, we had evening devotions. As Dad prayed, he prayed for the girls and us.

The house echoed with the quiet. I spent the evening moving from one task to the next and did not settle down to anything.

Thursday, November 20, 1947

It was cold and dreary all day. Is it the weather or my mood?

Mrs. B. called in sick. I do not know if she has ever missed a day of school.

At recess, a tearful Betty slipped me this note.

* * * * *

Miss Morland,

I am not allowed to talk to you or have anything to do with you ever again. If I do, I will get whooped on.

I will be your friend forever.

Betty

xoxoxoxoxo

P. S. I miss you.

P. P. S. I love you.

P. P. P. S. You are my best friend.

That explained why Lily and Rose and Violet were quiet, sullen, and un-friendly. They would not look at me. They answered only when called on.

Chicken and rice soup with carrot strips for supper.

Uncle Bob and Aunt Doris stopped in after supper. She brought a chocolate cake, so the four of us kept having one more piece until we had eaten over half of it. The talk was about our relatives, the girls, the church, the girls, crops, the girls, the high school football team, and the girls.

Aunt Doris and Uncle Bob have decided to join St. John's in Bancroft. It will be a bit of a drive, but they are not happy with the new building either. They feel the money could have been used more wisely.

Friday, November 21, 1947

Mrs. B. had called in sick so she could stay home and listen to the broadcast of Princess Elizabeth's wedding. That was all she has talked about for weeks. Janice asked her if she had been expecting an invitation. If looks could kill, Janice would be in the grave.

It is a long day with the girls refusing to answer or look at me. Betty slipped me a note again at recess.

* * * * *

Dear Miss Morland,

    I miss you.

    I miss your old dad.

    I miss your preacher man.

    I miss your smile.

    Mama is real mad. She had gone somewhere with a man who smelled real bad. He said he was going to come back for us. We would live on a farm and be happy forever.

    He hit her.

    She came home very mad. She drinks lots of medicine, and she lays in bed and sleeps. I wish she would go back to work.

    I wish I could come see you.

    We are all sad.

Betty

    P. S. I wish I could live with you forever.

Saturday, November 22, 1947

I needed to keep busy today, so I cleaned the house top to bottom and then baked bread and gingersnaps.

I still worried about the girls.

I even sat and listened to *Terry and the Pirates.*

The vicar showed up at supper time. We always tease him about his timing, and he usually seems to enjoy it. But today he was withdrawn.

Finally, over tea and gingersnaps, he told us. He was loading some freight in the depot's backyard, and he heard the most awful row coming from the Speck's house. The vicar went over to investigate. Someone must have called the sheriff because soon he also showed up. Some man was in the house slapping Mrs. Speck around. She was kicking and punching him. It took the sheriff and the vicar both to get them apart. Mrs. Speck started screaming and crying and hitting the sheriff and the vicar. There were empty liquor bottles all over the room.

All the while the girls were hiding under the bed.

The man, a shoe salesman, is now at the jail for disturbing the peace and will be leaving town the first thing in the morning. The sheriff told him that he would not press charges if he promised never to come back to Kingsbury County.

Dad and I sat stunned for a long time. These things just do not happen in De Smet. The vicar said he asked the sheriff about removing the girls from the situation. The sheriff did not give him much hope. He said it would have to get a lot worse before the law would step in.

Sunday, November 23, 1947

I am not sure if I slept at all last night. I was in bed, in the rocker, on the couch, back in bed. When Dad got up, he came into the kitchen and took one look at me and gave me a hug. Neither of us felt like being around people, so we stayed home from church.

We decided that sitting at home was not what we needed, so we took a drive. Watching the countryside speed by was calming. It was not long before we found ourselves in Huron. We ate supper at The Barn and drove home.

When we walked into the house, the phone was ringing, and the vicar was quite worried as he had not been able to find us all day.

Monday, November 24, 1947

After school I went to visit Mrs. Speck. I was told in very precise terms to mind my own business and to stay away. She threatened to knock me "flat as a panacake."

* * * * *

Andrew O'Brien
1900 Frank Str.
Aberdeen, So. Dak
November 24, 1947

Dear Hanna,
Your letter arrived on Friday, and I must say that I wanted to call and talk to you. I am so sorry about the girls, and that their mother has returned. I realize that is difficult for you.
Life is not always easy. But you know that already.
Thank you for the dark brown mittens you sent. The snowflake pattern that you knitted into them is beautiful. I have been snow-shoeing and skiing, so I have put them to good use.
We have had plenty of snow and I have been able to go to the slough and collect more specimens. This past week I snared a rabbit in its winter coat.
I hope your next week is blessed with joy. I look forward to hearing from you.
Sincerely,
Andrew O'Brien

* * * * *

Tuesday, November 25, 1947

Some of the vicar's mother's belongings arrived at the depot. He borrowed the pickup and took them to the farm. It was nice to see him so excited. He could barely contain his joy. I offered to come clean, but he said the house was clean and his mother would clean it again after she arrived.

Her arrival date is not yet set. It seems her employer was not willing to let her go until after Christmas.

Wednesday, November 26, 1947

I baked pumpkin pies and set the table for tomorrow. For the first time, since Mom went home, I used her best china. It is time.

The vicar came to see dad, and they were talking in hushed tones. I stayed in the kitchen.

* * * * *

Calvary Cathedral
Sioux Falls, South Dakota

Jacob,
 I am not coming to De Smet this week. I have no plans to talk to you. You will not see me as I will not be there.
      Sincerely,
      His Holiness,
      Bishop Bradbury

* * * * *

Thursday, November 27, 1947
Thanksgiving

So much has happened today, I hope that I do not forget any of it.

Of course, I was up early cooking for today's meal. I had the turkey in the oven by six. It is a huge one. I was still a bit worried that it would be enough.

Dad did not make it back, from choring, in time for church, so I walked to St. Paul's alone. I felt like a stranger in my own home. It is strange how these issues can divide people. I think I may have just gone along with the new building. I still have not been able to understand Dad's reaction completely. It seems so out of character for him. I hope shortly we can find a church home and settle in.

Mrs. Roberts had done a beautiful job decorating the church, so I thought I would complement her.

That was the wrong thing to do…her response was less than pleasant. She reminded me I was still a member of the altar guild, and I should have been helping her. She had to do it all by herself. She had a lot of work that needed to be done at home, but she left her work undone because church came first for her. She went on to tell me my mother would be so ashamed of my behavior, gallivanting all over the countryside chasing men.

I am not sure what got into me, but I forgot to be kind. I was unkind.

"Well, if you were not so busy minding everyone else's business you would have plenty of time to get your work done," I retorted.

This time Mrs. Roberts was speechless.

I felt withered, but I stood firm.

Our house quickly filled up with people, pleasant smells, smiles and hugs and laughter, the warmth of family and friends…a true holiday.

We had just sat down to eat when the doorbell rang. It was Andrew O'Brien. Quickly we made space for him. He has come for the weekend. He says he sent a letter, but I have not received it. It was so good to see him. When we shook hands, I had a hard time releasing his.

It was a pleasant afternoon. We played games. I played the piano, and we sang a while.

When Dad left to chore, the vicar left with him. The vicar was very quiet all afternoon. I wonder what is bothering him.

After supper we visited until quite late. Andrew is staying at the De Smet Hotel.

I am feeling cozy and content. The fuss with Mrs. Roberts is almost forgotten in my contentment. I wonder what makes her so critical and ready to hurt others. And why was I so willing to be unkind?

Friday, November 28, 1947

I slept in until seven. I picked up the house and put everything back to normal.

Andrew's letter telling me he was coming for the weekend arrived today.

Andrew worked on some school work in the morning at the hotel. He came for lunch, then we walked to the farm, and I showed him around.

In the evening we went to Spirit Lake for a skating party. The ice was not very thick yet, but we skated anyway. The men made a big bonfire, and we roasted wieners and sausages. The vicar was there but mostly kept to himself.

Andrew and I skated and sat by the fire. I like Andrew. He has a quiet confidence about him; he is very handsome with his dark hair and blue eyes.

Janice embarrassed us both by carrying on about his looks as only she can. "Willie" eyed her at a distance but was all smiles when she turned her attention back to him.

Saturday, November 29, 1947

Andrew and I drove to Brookings, walked up and down Main Street and the college campus.

Dad had gotten tickets to Billy Dean and the Missouri Valley Barn Dance. Mike and Marilyn and Dad met us at Nick's for burgers.

We were in our seats in the college auditorium by 7:30. At 8 P.M. the band came in to warm up. Right at 8:30, Billy Dean was live on WNAX. It was exciting.

Dad rode home with us. We were all tired so there was not much talking.

Sunday, November 30, 1947
The first week in Advent

We all rode with Andrew in his car to Lake Whitewood Lutheran for church. Afterward, we were invited to the Hollister's for dinner.

When we got home, Andrew left for Aberdeen. When he said goodbye, he held my hand in both of his for quite some time.

I was glad to see him come. I enjoyed my time with him. I was also glad to see him go. I am not sure how I feel about it all. He is very interested in me. I wish I could talk to Mom.

Monday, December 1, 1947

We woke up to more snow.

School has slipped into a nice routine. Lily and Rose and Violet have forgotten that they are not supposed to talk to me. The classroom is pleasant. There remains a fragile truce between Danny and Lily.

Betty slips me a note every day.

Wednesday, December 3, 1947

It was a beautiful sunny day. It was warm enough that the snow melted a bit. I was on recess duty and about a block away I saw Mrs. Speck and the bishop again. It was time to go in, but I became Nancy Drew again and hid behind a tree. I waited until they were close enough that I could be sure it was them and then ran quickly inside.

The vicar stopped by after work. He said that as the afternoon passenger train pulled in, he thought he saw the bishop on the train. He played Joe Hardy, hid behind the depot, and peered around the corner. He said that the bishop got off the train, looked around and made a beeline for the De Smet Hotel. He said he walked so quickly and that he waddled like a Keystone Cop from the movies.

Thursday, December 4, 1947

Another warm sunny day.

Joe Hardy stopped by after work to compare notes with Nancy Drew. From the depot, he saw Mrs. Speck walk to the hotel. He hid behind the post office and waited.

After a few minutes, Mrs. Speck and the bishop left the hotel with her arm linked through his.

Nancy had nothing more to report.

The vicar showed me a letter he had received from the bishop saying he was not going to be in De Smet, but he was there and seen by two detectives.

Friday, December 5, 1947

After school, I stopped by the hotel and fortunately Mrs. Thomas was working. We visited about the weather, her grandson, and then I mentioned that I had seen a gentleman in the company of Mrs. Speck, and they seemed to be enjoying this beautiful weather.

I felt guilty about leading her to gossip, but she told me lots. Nancy Drew must gather information in some way. Yes, he was a gentleman from Sioux Falls who came specially to see Mrs. Speck. He stays in his room, and has the diner deliver his food. He only leaves to go for walks with her.

Mrs. Thomas complained about the amount of time it takes to clean his room. She also says that he is a lousy tipper, and although you would think he was neat from the way he dresses, his room is a mess. He even used a clean towel to shine his shoes, and she had a lot of trouble getting it clean. He is always kissing Mrs. Thomas' hand, and she DOES NOT LIKE IT. She says he is a minister.

The vicar told me the bishop left on the afternoon train.

Saturday, December 6, 1947

The vicar called and asked if we wanted to go to Brookings to church with him. Dad said we would go with him; he has wanted to go back to St. Paul's in Brookings.

Sunday, December 7, 1947
The second week in Advent

The vicar's car did not start, so we went in the pickup. The heater did not keep up. It was cold; I was glad for the two warm bodies pressed against me. We laid a woolen robe across our laps. I brought a thermos of coffee, which also helped to keep us warm.

For the first time since Thanksgiving, the vicar seems to be himself.

Close to Arlington, I had to use the restroom so badly that every bump jarred me. We stopped at a farmhouse, and I made a beeline for their outhouse.

We made it to church just in time and slipped into a pew during the opening hymn.

The sermon was comforting, it was about resting in God, and He would take care of you. "Casting all your care upon him; for He careth for you" 1 Peter 5:7.

We were invited to the vicarage for dinner, which is right next door. The vicar's wife, Jane Howard, is a sweet woman and they have a lively houseful of five children. She served a thick stew and biscuits. She apologized for serving a simple meal, but since she set such a neat table and the company was so comfortable, it seemed far richer.

They have a fifth grader that reminds me of Betty. Quiet, shy, and intelligent. I asked her if she would like to have a pen pal. I think she and Betty could be great friends.

After dinner, the vicar told his story of receiving the letter and then seeing the bishop with Mrs. Speck. Rev. Howard said that was so unlike the bishop. The bishop is married and just would not be courting a woman in De Smet.

The vicar said that early on the bishop had insisted that he be addressed as "Your Grace," and he signs his letter "His Holiness."

Rev. Howard said, "That is so unlike the bishop, he is a humble man and would never feel comfortable with such a term of address. And anyway isn't "Your Grace" the British way to address a duke?"

I was so embarrassed when he told them of our spying on them. I could not believe he would do that. His eyes looked so jolly as he told them. He then went on to relate that we called each other Nancy Drew and Joe Hardy. This got such a laugh. Dad laughed so hard he had tears. I thought about acting put out but decided just to enjoy it.

The vicar and Rev. Howard then made plans to go to Sioux Falls together. If they took the morning train, they could be in Sioux Falls by noon and maybe return the same day.

Dad offered to work for the vicar at the depot.

As we drove away, the seven of them hollered out, "Goodbye Joe, Goodbye Nancy."

The ride home was as cold as this morning. When we were about at Hetland, it started snowing. It was nice to get home into our snug house.

The vicar took the pickup and did evening chores.

Dad thought himself as funny as Red Skelton; he called me Nancy all evening.

Monday, December 8, 1947

The vicar left on the early train.

Dad worked at the depot today and still did the chores. He brought home all the eggs for me to wash. I am amazed at how many we are still getting.

It flurried most of the day. Every chance the children got they were looking out the window, sighing and hoping for more snow.

At lunch, Janice was also complaining about her students, so we cooked up the idea of a talent show. Her class came into my room for the last hour. We had poems, songs, long recitations, and impersonations. In the middle of it, Mr. Warren came in, stood, and watched, then left.

After school, Mrs. B. came into my room. She started out by saying it is too bad the good teachers get in trouble and the lazy ones do not. She went on to tell me it was a good thing Janice was my friend; otherwise, I would have gotten another talking to by the principal.

* * * * *

1900 Frank Str.
Aberdeen, So. Dak
December 8, 1947

Dear Hanna,
I see from the weather report in the newspaper that you have also had plenty of snow this winter.

The next few weeks will be busy with semester finals, staff Christmas parties, and I have a few friends that are passing through on their way to a wedding in Wisconsin and they want to see me. They were in my unit in the air corp. I have not seen them since we were discharged. So, it will be good to catch up.

I will be going to Vermillion for Christmas. May I stop on my way home and see you?

What kind of traditions does your family have? I have been shopping for gifts for the family. It is hard to decide what they will like and use.

The Boarding House Gang all went to a Christmas concert at the Opera House. It was all a bit too high brow for me. Afterwards we went to Walgreens for floats. When we got home, Mrs. Baum had the dining room table set with coffee and cookies for us. Around midnight we waddled up to bed.

Thank you for sharing your excitement over your new reading curriculum. I am glad that you like it and have seen improvement in the children's reading. Growing up, our farm was too far from town, so we went to a country school. I had the same teacher for all eight grades—Mr. Hennesy. I would be very hard pressed to think of any child that did not receive the rod of correction. We were taught "by the tune of the hickory stick." He did instill in us a love of learning though.

Will your school have a Christmas concert? What are your Christmas plans for your classroom? What do you want Santa to bring you? I know what I want.

Sincerely,
Andrew O'Brien

* * * * *

Tuesday, December 9, 1947

The De Smet Ladies' Book Club met today. Mrs. Petersen was so kind and requested that it start at four so I could attend. We did not discuss a book, instead we had our Christmas party. Mrs. Peterson said she was not ready to decorate for Christmas, but she had put out so many lovely decorations that it felt very Christmassy. She had taken fir branches that were about two feet long and set them around in pots covered with gold foil. These branches were decorated with the tiniest glass balls. On the table in the living room, she had tumbleweed that she had dipped in whitewash and decorated with small red bows and tiny balls. She served coffee and a beautiful tearing. At the gift exchange, I got a nice box of stationery. Mrs. Danley seemed pleased with the copy of Emily Dickinson's poems that I gave.

At supper, the vicar called collect and told us he would be home tomorrow and had so much to tell us.

* * * * *

Jacob Stewart
Kensington Hotel
Sioux Falls, South Dakota

Bishop Taylor
St. John the Divine
New York, New York

Dear Bishop Taylor,

I hope this letter finds you in the best of health. Today, especially today, I missed our visits and your guidance.

I have a most interesting story to relate. It is an account of stolen identity, an account of coincidence, and divine appointment. My heart rejoices at the workings of God.

As you know, the man that I thought was the bishop had come to see me. I have gone to Sioux Falls to meet with him and not seen him there. I have sent numerous letters and made several long distance calls. I have visited with the area priests. All to no effect.

Last week, I received the oddest letter from the bishop. All his letters have been odd, but this was most odd. He wrote to tell me he was not coming to De Smet and that I would not see him. However, I did see him there on several occasions. Since I work at the depot, I saw him get off the train. I saw him on two occasions in the company of Mrs. Speck. (You may recall that Mrs. Speck is the mother of the four girls that have wormed their way into my life).

Miss Morland also saw him with Mrs. Speck on one occasion and visited with the hotel staff about him.

I will digress here. Miss Morland and I have become real live Nancy Drew and Joe Hardy with our following and investigating. We became quite adept at dodging behind trees as we followed our suspects.

Sunday last, Mr. Morland, Miss Morland, and I traveled to attend the morning service at St. Paul's Episcopal in Brookings. It is a college town about forty miles to the east.

Again, I digress; it was cold and the heater in their pickup was not able to keep up, but I was very warm. Being squeezed into the seat with Miss Morland pressed against me from shoulder to knee, kept me very warm.

We had a most pleasant time with Rev. Charles Howard and his family. I shared with him my latest letter from the bishop and that I had seen the bishop in the company of a woman several times. He found the whole story incredulous. He stated quite firmly that the bishop is happily married and would not court a woman elsewhere. We made plans to leave the next day for Sioux Falls.

When my train passed through Brookings, Rev. Charles Howard joined me. His kind wife, Jane, sent breakfast, knowing I would not have taken time to eat before boarding in De Smet.

Upon arriving at the station in Sioux Falls, we started walking to the Cathedral and Diocesan Offices. A block ahead, I spied the bishop, scurrying along in his customary bowler. I pointed him out to Charles, saying, "There is the bishop, should we catch up to him?" He said I was undoubtedly mistaken. Bishop Bradbury is tall, thin, and walks with a limp from his time of service.

We saw the man with the derby enter the Diocesan Offices.

Charles and I were greeted warmly by the bishop's secretary and shortly were shown into the bishop's office.

Yes, I am mistaken. Bishop Bradbury is a tall thin man. He stands well over six foot. He was warm and friendly; he carefully listened as I related my story. When I showed him the letters I had received from his office, a deep line creased his forehead. I could readily see why the neighboring priests kept telling me the behavior of the man that I had met was so unlike the bishop they knew. I told him of Ernst Morland and my traveling to Sioux Falls in June to visit with him.

He then ordered a cup of tea and shortbread for us and asked me to relate my story again this time adding more details. Charles joined in and even told him of my following the bishop and hiding behind buildings and trees. Bishop Bradbury found this humorous and laughed heartily.

Pressing the intercom, Bishop Bradbury asked his secretary to consult his diary and locate where they had been on June 10. They had indeed been visiting the parishes in the western part of the state and had left Verger Edwards in charge of the office. The bishop then requested the secretary ask Verger Edwards to come to his office. As the verger entered, he took one look at me and tried to bolt out the door. Divinely appointed time prevailed. At that moment, the secretary was walking in. They collided and ended up in a heap on the floor. I reached down and grabbed Verger Edwards by the ankle. Although he squirmed and kicked, I was able to keep him from leaving.

At first, he sat stone faced silent to the bishop's questioning. Slowly he belligerently answered the questions. He had opened the letters from you and had written to me. He had gone to De Smet and passed himself off as the bishop. He was glad that he had done it. If he had not, he would not have met a most beautiful woman who cares deeply for him.

Bishop Bradbury continued to inquire as to why he had done this. He would not answer until he finally blurted out that your first letter arrived opened, and he had accidentally read it.

He felt he deserved to be appointed Deacon and especially deserved the right to be the deacon in De Smet. He had been passed over so often for far less worthy men. He was tired of being treated as if he was not important, as if he were a lowly sexton. He was destined for greater things.

All the letters were in his desk and the secretary was dispatched to retrieve them. They were neatly wrapped in newspaper and tied with string.

At this the verger stood, mustered all the dignity he could, adjusted his clothing, and tendered his resignation, stating he was going to follow his heart and go to the lady he loved. He was going to marry her.

I asked him what his plan was for her four daughters. He told me I was sadly mistaken. His lovely woman did not have any chil-

dren, but they were going to let their love fully blossom and have a large family.

He then turned and left the room.

The rest is far less dramatic.

Bishop Bradbury apologized and has given me permission to open the church and commence services.

As we were leaving, he turned to me and said, "One last question young man. How did you get into the church originally? Was it unlocked?"

I told him that it was indeed locked when I got there. I decided that the people of De Smet were probably quite trusting and wondered where they would have hidden a key. Since I had permission to be there, I looked around and found the key hanging on the door frame.

We were invited to the bishop's house for supper. Tomorrow morning, we will visit with him and his secretary to learn more about the workings and finances of the congregation. We plan to leave on the afternoon train.

My dear sir, it is the unwinding of a very long day. I am exhausted, but I know I will not sleep from the excitement of it all.

I remain,

Your servant,

Jacob

* * * * *

Wednesday, December 10, 1947

I could hardly sleep last night. I kept wondering what the vicar had learned and what he would tell us.

School went at a snail's pace. I was on edge, and the children got on my nerves. I had a hard time being patient.

I stopped by Peschel's and got some ground pork and beef. For supper, I made Swedish meatballs, gravy, boiled potatoes, and beans, with canned peach pie for dessert.

The vicar arrived before Dad; it was so hard to wait. As soon as Dad was settled in, the vicar started his story. And then once he began his story, it was even harder not to interrupt and ask questions. His eyes were alive with delight as he related all that had happened.

It is so unbelievable, thinking of that little man posing as the bishop and causing so much trouble.

I do wonder about that little man thinking that Mrs. Speck does not have any children.

* * * * *

Jacob Stewart
General Delivery
De Smet, South Dakota
December 10, 1947

Bishop Taylor
St. John the Divine
New York, New York

My Dear Sir,

I am now ensconced at home. The last few days have been very exhilarating. I wanted to tell you a bit more of my trip to Sioux Falls.

We went to the bishop's house for supper and a lively discussion. He has asked Charles to mentor me since he is much closer.

With a handshake that ended in a warm embrace, he wished us Godspeed.

We decided on the fourth week in Advent for our dedication service. He and his wife will travel here.

I am glad you encouraged me to take the chance and go to see the bishop. I have been sleeping better.

Sincerely,
Jacob

* * * * *

Friday, December 12, 1947

Lily and Rose and Violet were quite agitated all day. They whispered and giggled but would not tell me what was going on.

The vicar called in the evening to tell us that the little man, Mr. Edwards, had arrived at the depot, and he had several crates and boxes in the boxcar that he wanted unloaded and delivered to Mrs. Speck's house. After making that announcement, he went directly to the De Smet Hotel.

So that must have been what was going on.

Saturday, December 13, 1947

When I got up, on the back porch was a shoebox, a cigar box, the books I had given Betty and a note. In the boxes were her dolls, her crocheting, and other girlish trinkets.

* * * * *

Miss Morland,

Mama's new boyfriend came to see us, and they got in an awful fuss. He did not know she had children.

He stomped out and said his heart was broken. She started drinking her medicine and got mad. We skedaddled out of there. We hid in the shed until she fell asleep.

If I never don't see you again, you will always be my best friend.

Please keep these things safe for me. I hope to come and get them soon.

Please tell your old dad and the preacher I love them too.

Love,

Betty

* * * * *

I went to the house, but no one answered the door. Mrs. Speck and Mr. Edwards were not at the hotel. Mrs. Thomas said that he had not checked out.

I love those little girls; however, they have caused so much worry and concern. I am sure Dad would say that is what love is all about.

Mrs. Allen picked me up. We went to the farm and cut spruce and cedar branches from the tree row to decorate the altar and make an advent wreath. I am sure our job was not as superb as Mrs. Walter's advent decorations, but we were satisfied.

Sunday, December 14, 1947
The third week in Advent

We went to St. Stephen's for Matins. We sang "O Come O Come Immanuel." Oh, it really rang in the rafters.

We were invited to the Gates' house for dinner and a pleasant afternoon. I took a basket of dinner rolls.

We went to the Speck's house twice and did not find anyone home.

After supper Dad helped me grade papers while we listened to the radio.

Monday, December 15, 1947

A cold wind blew all day. The weather fit my mood and with all that has happened.

Betty and Lily and Rose and Violet did not come to school. Irene called the sheriff to see if he would check on them. He said they had to be truant for a week before he could do anything.

So, I fretted and worried all day. Or rather, I have fretted and worried and suffered for the last four days.

Danny Vincent came up to me at the end of the day and said he missed "that stinky old Lily."

I started supper and decided to lie down a bit since I have not been sleeping well. I woke up to the house filled with smoke. Supper was ruined. I am not sure how I will ever get the pots clean.

Dad took pity on me, and we went to the Ritz Café.

Tuesday, December 16, 1947

Cold and still today. It dipped below zero. Dad came in with a huge smile and rubbing his hands. He called Michael to see if he would go ice fishing with him.

Dad asked around town about Mrs. Speck and Mr. Edwards. Mr. Edwards bought a car at O'Keeffe's and was seen loading it at Mrs. Specks. They had told the hotel manager they were going to move to Arizona.

Mrs. Thomas called and reported they told her that they planned to drop the girls off at an orphanage; they would have more of their own.

Wednesday, December 17, 1947

It was a bit warmer today.

There was no news from the girls.

Dad caught a perch, which I baked for supper with French fried potatoes and cabbage slaw.

We were just sitting down to eat when the vicar showed up. We got a good laugh about that. The only problem is that when he shows up like that, I do not have leftovers for Dad's lunch. Although, he does not seem to mind making a sandwich or going to the café.

The vicar asked if the bishop and his wife could spend the weekend with us. They will be driving up tomorrow. He also wondered who might keep the Howards and their five children.

After much discussion, it was decided that the bishop and his wife would stay at the farm and the seven Howards would fill our house. Dad offered to move to the farm and give up his room, but we decided the Bradburys might enjoy roughing it. The vicar said he thought they were just common folk and that a few days on the farm would not be too out of the ordinary.

Thursday, December 18, 1947

Dad worked at the depot for the vicar so he could spend time with the bishop.

I rushed home from school and worked feverishly getting supper on. I was still in my school dress, and my hair had come undone when they knocked at the front door. It was the vicar and the bishop and his wife.

Bishop and Mrs. Bradbury are so warm and comfortable they quickly put me at ease. They joined me in the kitchen; she donned an apron and helped get supper on.

The vicar got in the way trying to help by making tea. She swatted him and told him to sit down and let her handle it.

After supper, we all sat in the kitchen and visited.

Mrs. Bradbury asked if she could take a bath here. She did not mind staying at the farm, but a bath in a tub in the kitchen was not what she wanted to do.

Friday, December 19, 1947

Dad worked at the depot again. The vicar, the bishop, and his wife spent the day visiting with former members and inviting them to church.

At school, we spent the morning with the children working diligently on the gifts they are making for their parents.

While the children enjoyed a cup of hot chocolate and a few cookies, I gave them the gifts I bought in Aberdeen. They seemed pleased with the jacks and cars. I opened my gifts from them. I love to watch their shining eyes as they watch me. I got a lot of hankies and pencils and bars of soap. Then after afternoon recess, we assembled in the gym. We sang carols and Santa arrived with a paper bag filled with an apple, an orange, nuts, and candy for each child. For some of our poorer families, that will be their whole Christmas.

From Irene, I got a pixie doll pin cushion she had sewn. Rosanna gave Dad and me a coffee can full of peanut brittle. Janice came in waving an orange scarf to brighten up my "drab coat." Mrs. B. had taken old neckties and made a pillow for each of us. It was thoughtful. I had not thought of giving her a Christmas gift. I will need to think of something and drop it by her house next week.

The Howards came in the late afternoon. I had supper prepared, and Jane brought plenty more with her. She said she was used to feeding an army.

The sheriff showed up at supper time and Dad made room for one more at the table. Sometimes it feels like the miracle of the loaves and fishes around here.

The sheriff heard from the Children's Home Society. The girls had been dropped off there on Tuesday. He understood, from the Society, that Mrs. Speck and her new beau told them they will come to get them or send for them in a few months. I do wonder if they ever will.

By Thursday noon, Betty and Lily and Rose and Violet had run away. All the sheriff's departments between Sioux Falls and De Smet have been notified to be on the watch for them.

With these winter temperatures, I am somewhat beside myself.

At evening devotions, Dad prayed for them.

Saturday, December 20, 1947

Mrs. Bradbury and I were in the St. Stephen's church basement kitchen making pies for tomorrow's dinner when we heard Melvin Wiese talking to the bishop and the vicar in the fellowship hall upstairs. We did not even need to eavesdrop. He is such a loud man that we clearly heard every word. He started out talking very friendly. The vicar introduced him to the bishop, and he asked if there was a new bishop, because he had met and had spoken to another one. Bishop Bradbury brushed it off with a comment that everything is new now. Melvin Wiese then started talking loudly about how he and the other bishop had decided this church should close and the members join up with "my church." He said he strongly feels that everyone should join in support of building the new church. It was God's will.

The vicar tried to talk to him, and Melvin Wiese just kept on talking and not listening. They stood and listened until he ran out of steam. Then Bishop Bradbury, in a kind way, told him they felt it was God's will to open this church and he was welcome to disagree.

He then started shouting. "You don't think this bearded wonder could lead a congregation, do you?"

The bishop replied, "Not only do I think this bearded wonder can lead a congregation, but I also think he will do an outstanding job. I also think he makes an excellent detective." The two of them started laughing, and Melvin Wiese stomped out.

The rest of the day was spent getting the church ready for tomorrow. The tables are set, the silver and dishes washed, and the windows are spotless. A real spirit of celebration filled the church today.

As I was getting ready to walk home, the vicar asked me if I wanted to see the room he lived in before moving to the farm. It is a tiny room in the basement, so very dark and damp. He then walked me home. As we walked, his hand brushed against mine several times. I wondered if he wanted to take mine. But he did not.

The rest of the evening was lively with getting all the Howards bathed and to bed. Jane does it all with a smile.

Sunday, December 21, 1947
The fourth week in Advent

A cold, bright, sunny Sunday.

Rev. Howard left early for the church. Jane, her brood, Dad, and I went later. As we walked, the children started singing Christmas carols. We marched in time to "O Come All Ye Faithful."

Mrs. Allen had added more greens, which made the church seem so Christmassy. She had a tree standing near the altar.

Everyone was in a festive mood. There were twenty-five in attendance; thirty-four including the Howards and Bradburys.

The vicar and Rev. Howard shared the liturgy, and Bishop Bradbury had the sermon. We were encouraged to look to the shepherds and their example and to go and tell what we have heard from the angels.

There was communion and a long prayer of rededication for the church.

Then we all trooped to the fellowship hall and ate a basket dinner. Jane leaned over and told me to "look at your vicar." The vicar looked as if he were ready to cry. And yet, he was beaming all over. I then noticed he was wearing his new suit. He looked quite handsome in it. Although I am going to have to let it out, it is a bit tight across the back.

With lots of hugs and promises to keep in touch, the Bradburys and the Howards left for home. The vicar came over for supper and was just content to sit and not talk. When he left, he said his cup runneth over.

Monday, December 22, 1947

It is cold; the temperature stayed around zero today. There is still no word of the girls.

Tuesday, December 23, 1947

The same as yesterday. I am nervous and skittish.

Wednesday, December 24, 1947
Christmas Eve

The vicar's mother arrived on the morning train; the man she cleaned for decided she should be with her son for Christmas. The vicar was going to take her to the farm and bring her back for supper, but the sheriff called and said the girls had been seen around Freeman. He hurriedly left to see if he could find them.

Mrs. Stewart is a large woman but puts me in mind of a finch. She moves about with quick, lively movements.

She went upstairs to rest and came down in time for lunch. Dad wanted to do extra chores so he would not have so much to do tomorrow. I did not see him until supper.

Most of the day, I was left alone with Mrs. Stewart. At first, it was silent, and I racked my brain for something to talk about. But when she asked me about Betty and Lily and Rose and Violet, we had lots to talk about. She told me the vicar has never really shown much interest in children and she was surprised he was so taken up with them.

The vicar called collect about 9 o'clock. He had not found the children but had talked to a farmer that had seen them walking down the road.

A cold, hard, northwest wind came up at bedtime. It really shook the house when it hit.

Thursday, December 25, 1947
Christmas Day

We woke up to a massive blizzard. The radio said this was a most unusual snowstorm; phone lines are down all over. The weather forecasters did not see it coming. The eastern states were especially hit. Much of New York City is without power. Dad was glad he did extra chores yesterday. I am worried about getting out to the farm.

We still have no word from the vicar. The sheriff stopped in to see if we had heard anything. He said the trains were stalled over east by Tracy. He drank a cup of coffee and ate a sandwich and went back out in the storm.

We stayed in the kitchen and kept warm by the stove. None of us wanted to celebrate. All the food I had prepared will be saved until the vicar and the children are here.

If they ever are.

Friday, December 26, 1947

The wind blew all day until 3 P.M. Then as suddenly as it began, it stopped. It was silent. Dad quickly left for the farm.

Mrs. Stewart and I just sat and worried. She tried to remind me to be calm and trust the Lord. But I think she was as concerned as I was. I could not concentrate on handwork or read or anything. I cleaned and sat and worried and cleaned and sat and worried.

Dad had a lot of trouble getting to the farm. The pickup got stuck, and he ended up walking the last half mile there, and all the way home. He was frozen when he got back here. I sent him to bed with a hot toddy and a hot water bottle.

Saturday, December 27, 1947

This was a long day. People are slowly digging out. I heard the train whistle, so the trains came through today. They had over 26 inches of snow in New York City.

It was cold and clear. Mr. Gates came to pick up Dad and then they pulled the pickup out of the snow.

It was a day of worrying and baking and worrying and baking. When Dad came in for supper, he looked at all the baked goods and said, "Well at least one good thing comes from all your worrying."

We did not hear from the vicar until 8 o'clock when he walked in the back door. I ran to him, clung to him, and said, "Jacob, you are here."

Then the girls came crowding in, and everyone was talking at once. I quickly served them some supper and sat spellbound as they all told their story, laughing and interrupting each other.

After supper and baths the girls were ready to settle down for the night. As they were drifting off to sleep, Lily wondered if Santa would be coming yet, since they had missed him.

"I do not know about Santa, but I do know that the *Jul nisse* will be here sometime soon, so you had better go to sleep," was my response. I have a lot to get done by morning.

Sunday, December 28, 1947

After a good night's sleep, we were all ready to celebrate Christmas. The girls tumbled down the stairs with far more noise than was necessary. I told them they had to wait until after church and dinner to open their gifts.

Only the people that could walk to church made it. We had a joyous service.

Even though they could see the gifts stacked on the buffet, the girls kept asking about the *Jul nisse* and if he had come. They were quite disappointed when Dad told them the *Jul nisse* only brings presents to girls that speak Norwegian. Lily wanted to know then if all the gifts piled up were for me.

Mrs. Stewart suggested they open the gifts before the dishes, so we did. Betty and Lily and Rose and Violet were so pleased with the dolls and the clothes I had made.

Jacob was pleased with the devotional I had bought at Kaufmann's for him, *My Utmost for His Highest.*

Dad brought in a box wrapped in a feed sack. It was a used Featherweight Singer. He bought it last summer at Mr. Kaufmann's. It really purrs.

I gave Mrs. Stewart one of Peggy's rugs, she seemed pleased.

For supper we ate leftovers in the kitchen. The girls were very subdued. I think they were wondering about their mother. Among the adults the talk turned to Christmases past. Mrs. Stewart asked how we had celebrated Christmas when I was growing up. I stammered to answer, but Dad told her of celebrations on the farm and how much Mom loved Christmas. How she would look for or make small gifts for so many different people.

When the Stewarts left, I went up for a nap and found a wrapped gift on my nightstand. It was a photo album, with a wooden cover, which had bouquet of iris burnt into it and painted purple. And there was a note from Jacob thanking me for my friendship and all that I had done for him during the last year.

** * * * **

Jacob Stewart
De Smet, South Dakota
December 28, 1947

Bishop Taylor
St. John the Divine
NYC

My dear Sir,

The last few weeks have been full. I wrote to you about the dedication service but failed to fill you in on all the rest that has happened.

I would suggest you make yourself a cup of tea and sit back and rest before you read this. It threatens to be a long letter.

Verger Edwards came to De Smet and claimed the love of his life, Mrs. Speck. He did not know that she had four lively girls. That caused quite a bit of trouble between the two of them. He threatened to leave her. She somehow convinced him to take her to Arizona. Enroute, they left the girls at The Children's Home Society in Sioux Falls. I understand they told the Society that they would return for them once they were established in Arizona.

The girls ran away after two days. With their independent streak, the structure of the Society was not for them. The Society did outfit them in new clothes and winter gear, so they did have more when they left than when they arrived.

Their story is that they wandered around Sioux Falls for a few days, finding food where they could and staying in churches at night.

After asking around, they found out there were trucks that un-loaded cattle and hogs at the stockyards. The girls reasoned that any farm truck would be going to De Smet. When the driver was not looking, they got on a farm truck and stayed with it until he arrived home. The girls were almost frozen from riding in the open truck. The farmer took them in, and for a few days they stayed with him and his family. Rose had caught cold and was not able to travel. They ended up calling the doctor to look at her.

One night Betty heard them whispering that when Rose was well, they needed to return them to the Society.

That night they slipped out and started walking. They got as far as the neighbor's barn, where they spent the rest of the night and part of the next day. That afternoon, Betty was caught stealing food, and the girls were taken into the house. This family cared for them and called the sheriff the next day.

But again, Betty was able to get the girls out and away from that farm. They were seen a few times in the neighborhood walking along the road.

The county sheriff called our sheriff and told him they had been seen along the road near Freeman.

That was such an eventful day for me. Mother arrived on the morning train. I was able to pick her up and take her to the Morland's house before I left to look for the girls in Freeman, which is a farming community about 70 miles south of De Smet. I made good time in my Ford.

I stopped at the sheriff's office, but he did not know where they were, so I started driving aimlessly around the country. It was only by chance that I found them in a ditch huddled together. It did not take any convincing to get them in the car.

I drove to Freeman, and the sheriff sent us to the Lutheran min-ister. This was late Christmas Eve. The wind was blowing, and it had started to snow. They convinced us to spend the night. We were treated well, far better than Mary and Joseph were treated that first Christmas night. The good pastor's wife got all the girls bathed and cleaned up and looking far more presentable. We were fed and offered beds on the floor.

It was not long until the girls were sleeping with me and on me. It was not cozy. But they needed the assurance of someone they knew.

The next morning it was apparent we were not going anywhere. The phone lines were down, and a blizzard was raging.

I struggled through the snowstorm to the sheriff's office hoping there would be some way to get news to Mother and the Morlands. It was only a few blocks away, but I had tough going. The sheriff said there was no way to get news to them until the roads were clear or the phone lines were restored.

We spent the next two days waiting for the storm to stop and the roads to clear. Finally, on the 27th, we were able to start for home. With lunch prepared and our courage high, we left for home. We were about a mile from town when Betty suggested we should pray. Lily said, "Yeah a preacher should know that." We stopped and prayed.

The roads were not well cleared. We got stuck several times. Once, I had to leave the girls and walk to a farmhouse for help. After a long day, we finally arrived home at 8 in the evening.

But here my dear sir, I must tell you the most miraculous of things. I do not think that Miss Morland has ever used my Christian name; she has always called me Vicar. When I stepped in the back door, she came and threw her arms around me, and said, "Oh, Jacob, you are home safe."

While we ate supper and the girls related their adventures, I sat in stunned silence.

What does that mean?

My dear friend, I trust all is well with you and that you had a blessed Christmas season.

I remain,
Your servant,
Jacob

* * * * *

Monday, December 29, 1947

Right after breakfast, Betty asked for fabric scraps and started making her own Raggedy Ann and Andy. Lily and Rose and Violet were not to be outdone and asked me to make rag dolls for them. We spent a cozy day sewing and cutting and talking to our dolls.

Tuesday, December 30, 1947
Name Day celebration for people named David

Somehow Jacob found out that it was David's Name Day. He arranged for Marilyn to take the girls for the day and brought in lunch for us. He started by saying he knew it was hard for us to talk about David. But he wanted to get to know him and that part of our lives. We sat in silence for a few moments and then it was as if a dam had burst. We could not talk fast enough. We told of silly childhood things, his dreams of serving his country, his sweethearts, his ideas for building up the farm, and we introduced David to Jacob through our memories.

Wednesday, December 31, 1947
New Year's Eve

I spent the morning making a crown cake for tomorrow. I have not made *kransekake* since Mom died. I had forgotten how much work goes into making one. It turned out beautifully.

Jacob called after lunch and wondered if I wanted to go to the Grange with him tonight. That set my heart aflutter.

I called Jane Howard to ask how a vicar acts at a dance. She said Charles does not dance except a few waltzes. I honestly cannot see Charles or Jacob jitterbugging. But then again, I cannot see myself jitterbugging either.

I need to get dressed, but I wanted to write in here, as I think I will be too tired to do so later.

I have much to be thankful for this year: a new friend, I was able to take two college classes, a good crop of wheat, and Aunt Julia has a softer heart.

My resolutions from last year were to read the Bible through; be kind; and learn to control my temper. I read the Bible through, but I do not think I will ever learn to be kind or control my temper.

This coming year, I want to again work on learning to be kind and controlling my temper.

Thursday, January 1, 1948
New Year's Day

I slept in and took two naps. I am too old to go to New Year's Eve dances and to stay up until two in the morning.

I got up and got Dad and the girls' breakfast and then napped. Got up in time to make lunch and napped again. The girls were so thoughtful and played quietly or else I was so tired I just never heard them.

I finally felt rested and got up and bathed and then started on supper.

Jacob and his mother arrived on time. I made vegetable soup and rice pudding and served the crown cake with coffee. Everyone announced the *kransekake* was the best they had ever eaten. Except for Dad, it was the first time for all of them.

* * * * *

Jacob Stewart
General Delivery
De Smet, South Dakota
January 1, 1948

Bishop Taylor
St. John the Divine
New York City, New York

My dear friend,

It has been an eventful year, and I want to thank you for your part in it. You were far away; however, you have been supportive and a gentle guiding force.

I am sitting in the farmhouse, the oven is open, and the room is pleasantly warm. Mother is sitting and knitting. Her feet are up, and she has a rosy glow to her cheeks. She is adjusting well to life in the country.

The Speck girls have settled in nicely with the Morlands. It was quite an adventure to bring them home. The sheriff has tried unsuccessfully to contact their mother. I honestly wonder if she will ever come back for them.

Yesterday morning one of my friends, Mike, stopped by the depot and suggested that Miss Morland and I attend a dance at the Grange with him and his wife. I did not know if a dance was the place for me. I also did not know if Miss Morland would even consider going with me.

Mr. Wilke, the station master, joined in goading me. Your previous advice and my baser nature took over; I had to take their dare. When she answered the phone, I stammered and asked her to go with me. I was caught completely off guard when she accepted.

I picked her up at seven. Her dad opened the door. She came in from the kitchen with the little girls surrounding her. I do not have the words to describe her beauty or how I felt.

The dance was pleasant only because I was spending time with Hanna. I did try to dance a few waltzes with her. Once we got over our nervousness, we did marginally well. The band began a polka and she looked at me with her eyebrows up in a question. I stepped on her feet several times. We decided we were thirsty.

At midnight when all the other couples were kissing, we stood awkwardly and looked at each other. I extended my hand and thanked her for being my friend. She told me she was glad we had become friends. I wish I had the courage to tell her that I wanted to be more than friends.

I walked her to her door at 2 A.M. She said good night, opened the door and went in. I think she is content with being just friends.

Sir, I took the first step as you advised and asked her on a date. I am not sure what the next step is. She did not seem too averse to the first date. Dare I ask her on another date? She has started calling me Jacob all the time instead of Vicar. I take that as a good sign.

Epiphany and visiting with the members will fill my calendar. I continue to work at the depot as the congregation cannot yet afford a full time minister.

So far, Mother does not mind the primitive conditions of the farmhouse. I hope she will make friends and feel at home here. Perhaps in the spring, we should make a trip to New York to visit. I would enjoy seeing you again.

I trust all is well with you.

Most sincerely,

Jacob

* * * * *

Friday, January 2, 1948

Shortly after lunch Andrew knocked at the door. He had been visiting his parents and was on his way back to Aberdeen. I invited him in and gave him a cup of coffee. We talked. As we talked, Marilyn's words came true; she had said this thing with Andrew would become clear. I realized that although there was a lot about him I liked, he was not the one for me. Before he left, I told him I thought we should no longer write, and I was sure he would find someone closer to home. Oh, he looked so pained; it was all I could do to keep from crying.

I went to school and tried to get ready for next week, but my mind was not on it. I mostly sat and wondered if I had made the right decision.

Saturday, January 3, 1948

House cleaning, laundry, and baking. It is more work with four little girls to teach how to work and do a job well. Betty jumps right in and does a neat, careful job. It takes quite a bit to motivate Lily and Rose and Violet.

When Dad left to chore, we went with him and tried sledding down the hill by the creek. It was fun and we were able to be outdoors, which was good.

Jacob was in the kitchen waiting for us when we got back to town. He asked to talk to Dad while we listened to *Terry and the Pirates.* After a bit, Dad came in and told me Jacob wanted to talk to me. I had just made a pot of tea, so I took him a cup.

He was sitting as far away from the kitchen as possible and looked as nervous as I was. He told me he had apologized to Dad for asking me out without his permission and wanted to apologize to me also. "Would you be willing to go on another date with me?"

"Yes, I suppose, I would be willing for *one* more date."

"Would you go to Bryant to the movie with me tonight?" He was still in his work clothes and needed to go home, but if we hurried, we would make it in time for the late show.

Gentleman's Agreement was very interesting. On the way out, he held my hand.

Sunday, January 4, 1948

We were invited to Mrs. Callahan's for dinner. I took some of the butter horns that I made yesterday. Her grandchildren were there to entertain the girls.

Monday, January 5, 1948

School started back up. It will be good to be in a routine. The last week with the girls has been difficult. Between teaching them to entertain themselves and keeping up with all the work, I am worn out.

Mrs. B. came up to me at lunch and said, "You are a fool for dating that preacher. You'll always be poor as church mice."

Tuesday, January 6, 1948
Epiphany

Jacob had a short prayer service that we attended. It was just the Gates family and us.

Thursday, January 8, 1948

Jacob called and asked what we were going to do tomorrow evening. He suggested that instead of a movie, we could spend Saturday in Brookings and see if the Howards would invite us for dinner.

Saturday, January 10, 1948

Dad stayed with the girls so Jacob and I could go to Brookings. I am not sure if Dad minded or not. After a bit of shopping, we went to the Howards. Jacob had called them yesterday and they welcomed us with open arms. It was nice to sit and visit with Jane; she is so common. We had a nice conversation until she wanted to know all about our "romance," as she called it.

The wind picked up in the afternoon and it started to snow, but we made it back home shortly after supper. Dad had brought Mrs. Stewart home with him after chores. After living in New York City, I wonder if she is adjusting to life on the farm and away from all that activity. She reads a lot and does handwork, so she keeps busy.

Monday, January 12, 1948

The phone rang after supper; it was Jacob. When he was walking home from work, Hiram's big dog stood in the way and would not let him pass by. Jacob tried walking around him several times, all for naught. Eventually he heard a noise and went to investigate. While feeding his chickens, Hiram had gotten his feet tangled up in some fencing wire and had fallen. He could not get up and had lain there all day. Jacob helped him into the house but thought he should come into the hospital.

Dad went out and they took him to the hospital. He has pneumonia and will be staying there for a while.

Friday, January 16, 1948

Jacob took me to supper at the Ritz Café and afterwards we played Scrabble with Dad and Betty.

My mind was not on the game and several times Dad asked me what I was daydreaming about. One time when he asked, I looked at Jacob and he was blushing. I guess we were thinking of the same thing. I could hardly tell Dad that when Jacob brought me home, he had asked if he could kiss me before we went in. To make matters worse, Betty even spelled the word kiss.

Saturday, January 17, 1948

The Girls met at Barbara's to exchange the friendship quilt blocks we made. Some of them really got creative. I felt guilty as I did all my blocks in stem stitch. I plan to set my blocks in green sashing.

Of course, they all wanted to know about my dating the vicar and when we were getting married. Sad to say, I did enjoy being the center of attention.

I told them they were almost as silly and giggly as when we were in junior high and all of us had a crush on Gary Cooper. Barbara left and returned with a picture of him. We had all stood in line at the theater for an hour to get one. I reminded them that when our parents told us we could not go see him in *Mr. Deeds Goes to Town,* we cooked up the story that we were going to practice a song for school but went to the movie instead. I was grounded for a month.

Monday, January 19, 1948

Hiram was released from the hospital and will be staying with us until he gets his strength up. I will put him in the spare room on the main floor, where he will be close for us to care for him. If we get company, that leaves only one empty bedroom.

Friday, January 23, 1948

The sheriff came to see me at school and asked when he would be able to talk to Dad and me without the girls. He had received a letter from the Children's Home Society and wanted to talk to us about it.

Saturday, January 24, 1948

When Dad went to chore, he dropped the girls off at Marilyn's for the day. The sheriff and Jacob came for lunch. I served split pea soup, biscuits, and apple pie.

Sheriff Gearig seemed quite sad as he read aloud the letter from the Children's Home Society. The letter stated the Society had contacted Mrs. Speck when the girls were missing and again when they were found. They had written to tell her the girls were staying with us. Mrs. Speck had written back that she wanted them at the Society and locked up better so they could not run away again. She would be coming for them in the spring. The Society requested they be returned to Sioux Falls as soon as possible.

He asked us to draft a letter explaining why living with us was the best place for them, as they would run away from anywhere else. He also said that with winter weather and roads and all the crime in the county he would probably not have time to return them for a while. He had contacted the State's Attorney, who felt time was on our side; and recommended we react slowly. The county also sent a bill to the Society for the man hours used to search for the girls.

It is quite a letdown, but I guess we could not have planned on them staying with us forever. I wanted to write to Mrs. Speck, but the sheriff did not advise it. He thinks the less we have to do with her the better. He also thinks she will not come back for the girls.

After supper, Dad explained to the girls that they would eventually have to return to the Children's Home Society. Right away, Lily said, "Don't they know we will just run away?"

At devotions, Betty requested we pray that God will let them live with us.

Sunday, January 25, 1948

I did not sleep well last night. After I was in bed, Betty came to my room and wanted to talk. I let her crawl in bed with me. She does not want to return to the Society and says she has never been happier than she is with me and my "old dad." Through her tears she offered to live with us as our slave, just so she would not have to live with her mom or at the orphanage. She poured out her heart and told me about all her mother's boyfriends. She sobbed as she told me of one that hit her mother. Betty tried to stop him; he threw her against the wall. That was when she lost the use of her arm. She fell asleep in my arms.

The Stewarts were here for lunch and stayed all afternoon. It is becoming our Sunday habit to spend it with them. Mrs. Stewart is warm, but I am not sure if she approves of Jacob and my dating. And I am not going to ask her.

Tuesday, January 27, 1948

Hiram must be feeling better. He has become quite demanding with asking for certain dishes and likes to have his coffee cup full at all times. The girls like playing nurse, so that helps. Betty plays checkers with him by the hour.

Friday, January 30, 1948

Hiram moved back home today.

Saturday, January 31, 1948

All the young people met at Spirit Lake to skate. We had a nice bonfire and made hobo suppers in Dutch ovens.

When Schultzie showed up in his flivver and made it backfire, Jacob tensed up; he grabbed my hand and held on for dear life. When his breathing slowed to normal, he loosened his grip.

Later, I heard Michael talking to Schultzie about it. But Schultzie will never understand; he lives his life from one silly moment to the next.

On the way home, I wanted to ask Jacob what he thinks and feels during those times, but decided it was best for him to tell me when he is ready. My place is to be there for him.

Monday, February 2, 1948

If it does not rain, it pours. Janice stopped in after school and told me her Willie had asked the school board for permission to marry. The wedding will be Friday afternoon at the Methodist minister's house. As if I did not have enough to do, she asked me to stand up with her and make the wedding supper.

I said I would do it, but I was not thinking kind thoughts. I will just wear my dark blue wool dress; I do not have time to sew a new one.

Thursday February 5, 1948

I spent the evening preparing as much as I could for tomorrow's supper. Jacob stopped by after work. Seeing all the work in the kitchens, he went home and got his mother. I wanted to make this wedding a bit festive, so I invited all the teachers and school board to stop in, after supper, for cake and coffee.

I put Mrs. Stewart in charge of the hot water cakes. I hope three will be enough. I have the coleslaw made, the potatoes peeled, and the table set.

Betty helped me, while Dad helped by listening to the radio and playing games with Lily and Rose and Violet.

Friday, February 6, 1948

Shortly after lunch, Janice's parents arrived. If anyone looks like Ma and Pa Kettle it is her parents, only in reverse, he is large, and she is tiny. He was wearing bib overalls and she had on a flour sack dress. They are not at all happy about this event.

Dad took charge of entertaining them.

Janice had asked for the afternoon off. Mrs. B. had a lot to say about that, Janice was scheduled for recess and door duty and Mrs. B. had to do both. During afternoon recess, Mrs. B. came to my room and told me that when the minister asks if anyone has anything against the marriage I should speak up and request Mr. Warren marry me instead.

I could not figure out if she was serious or making a joke.

I rushed home after school to find Mrs. Stewart at the house working on supper. The roast was in, the cakes frosted, and everything was on time.

I barely had time to bathe before Jacob arrived to pick me up. He looked so handsome in his suit. I wonder how long it will be before he asks me to marry him.

We arrived at the minister's house. His wife met us at the door with an apron on, but quickly removed it.

Janice looked lovely. Mr. Warren had bought her a corsage of red and white rose buds. He kept wringing his hands.

The wedding was short—10 minutes—no scripture, nor prayer, nor hymns. The minister, his wife, Janice's parents, Jacob, and I were all that were in attendance.

At supper and afterward, her parents sat silently and almost appeared to fade into the background. Her mother wore a different flour sack dress, and her father was still wearing his bib overalls, but he had on a clean shirt.

Quite a few teachers and all the school board came after supper. I was glad there was enough cake.

Before she left the house, Mrs. B. told me I was a fool for letting Mr. Warren go. I looked across at Jacob and knew I was not a fool, but very blessed.

Saturday, February 7, 1948

To have a few minutes alone, I walked to the post office. Mr. Wiese and Mrs. Roberts were there. I really need to avoid the post office. Mr. Wiese did not speak or look at me. But Mrs. Roberts had plenty to say.

She has written Aunt Julia, "the only one with a lick of sense in the family," to express her concern about the way Dad and I have been behaving. I was not kind. To think of Aunt Julia as the only one in the family with sense! It struck me as so funny I started giggling and could not stop. I finally had to excuse myself and leave. I was a few blocks away before I realized I had forgotten the mail.

They were still in there talking when I returned. That just set me to laughing again.

The girls and I went skating in the afternoon.

Friday, February 13, 1948

Jacob came, after work, to visit with me. He seemed rather nervous. After giving each of the girls a nickel and sending them out to play we settled down to a cup of tea and snickerdoodles. He had a piece of paper that he kept folding and unfolding, but he never read it.

Rose interrupted by running in and yelling, "Come quick, Lily is dead!" She was not dead. She lay in the snow with her leg at a weird angle and had the wind knocked out of her. She had decided to ski off the garage roof. Jacob picked her up and carried her in. He thought she had broken her leg.

Well, the visit from the doctor confirmed it. He will set it tomorrow at his office. She is now enthroned in the living room on the couch, with her three Ladies in Waiting waiting on her every whim.

Jacob never did tell me what he had come for.

After everyone was in bed, I found the paper Jacob had been holding. It was a list of all the reasons why we should not marry and a list of reasons why we should. At first, I thought that I should drive out and talk to Marilyn but decided I can handle this on my own.

Saturday, February 14, 1948

Today would have been busy enough without having to take Lily to the doctor. Jacob came and helped carry her to the car and into the office. After the leg was set and she was given crutches, the doctor said she did not need to be carried, which caused quite a bit of pouting.

Tonight, was the annual auxiliary basket auction at the VFW. I made a simple basket with roast beef sandwiches, three bean salad, potato salad, lemon carrot salad, and chocolate cake.

I cannot believe my father! He slipped Schultzie $5 and told him to buy Mrs. B.'s basket. When her basket came up for sale, she looked at Dad, letting him know it was hers. As soon as the bidding started, Schultzie shouted, "Ten dollars!" No one bid against him, and he ate dinner with Mrs. B. She sat there with her eyes narrowed and arms crossed.

The bidding for my basket was not nearly as wild as last year, for which I am glad. Sheriff Gearig was competition for a bit but gave up at $2.00. Schultzie, thinking he was funny, then bid it up to $3.00. The baseball team started goading Jacob and bidding against him. He paid $9.25 to eat with me. I found a spot and laid out the meal.

When he had taken the first bite of his sandwich, I handed him his list and said, "Oh, you dropped this when you were at the house yesterday."

Choking on his mouthful and turning bright red, he looked at his list and then at me and then the list and then the ceiling and then the list and then me and sputtered and choked some more.

Not being a kind person, I could only smile.

"Can we talk about this later?" he stammered.

"Aunt Julia says it is best to meet things head on."

"I would really rather wait."

"I suppose we can."

"Thank you," he choked out.

Instead of taking me right home, he drove past our place and out to Spirit Lake. The moon made a silver path across the ice. We sat in silence for a long time; I could hear his irregular and shallow breathing.

Finally, he took out his list and read to me all the reasons we should not marry. He was poor, he did not even have a house for us to live in; he had to care for his mother; I could find a far finer man; and his time in the war had left him broken.

Then he read the reasons why we should marry. "I have loved you from the first day I saw you, and you fill an empty hole in my heart." Then with a smirk he added, "You are fairly good looking, you are a passable cook, you could possibly have children, you own land, and you are *now* attending the right church."

Very tentatively he said, "Hanna, I do not have a lot to offer, only my heart. Will you marry me?"

"Jacob, the war, and death had left me empty and without a future. You fill that emptiness and give me hope in a future. I will marry you."

"But what about the girls?" I added.

"They will always have a home with us."

* * * * *

Sunday, April 12, 1953

A pleasant Sunday. Jacob's sermon was well received this morning.

We met Mike and Marilyn at Spirit Lake for a picnic lunch. The children played so well together. That is except for Lily, she is such a scrapper. Betty and Shelly watched our Johanne and Graham, so that Marilyn and I could go wading and catch up. It seems as if we hardly ever see each other anymore. My little family and the church keep me very busy.

The men solved the world's problem and plotted out their plays for this summer's baseball team.

In the evening, Betty went to a young people's gathering. Dad and Mother Stewart spent the evening with us listening to the radio and working on a puzzle.

Jacob has Graham settled down and in bed.

I need a cup of tea. If Jacob has not fallen asleep, perhaps we can sit and talk.

* * * * *

Acknowledgments

I would like to express my indebtedness and gratitude to the many people for their support and assistance:

- my wife
- my family
- my friends
- my Beta readers
- April Rusche for her artwork used for the cover
- my writing group, James River Writers
- Dane for his editing and encouragement
- Lowell and Lee Printing for their patience and excellent formatting

I hope that you have enjoyed reading my book. If you would be so kind as to post a response on Amazon, Goodreads, or my Facebook page J.W. Jesser, I would appreciate it.

J. W. Jesser is a retired schoolteacher, father, and grandfather. He lives and gardens in rural South Dakota with his wife. This is his debut novel.

9 798989 503506